"I told you to leave .... House, Neita."

Fenn gazed at her, his green eyes cloudy. "You refused. Now that you've learned how dangerous it is for you to be around me, I hope you've changed your mind. Go home, Neita." His voice was hoarse now. "Go, before it's too late."

There was no denying she was tempted to leave, even though she had no fear of Fenn at this moment. What should she do? Why did she feel so positive that she and she alone could save him? This instinctive sense of hers was as intense as it was inexplicable. Even though she didn't yet understand what he must be saved from, she knew that if she deserted him now, she would never forgive herself.

She laid her hand on his arm, stunned by the thrill that quivered through her at the touch. "It's already too late, Fenn...."

Dear Reader,

They're spooky and they're creepy—but they'll never make you sleepy! They're our newest Shadows titles, guaranteed to keep you awake, reading—and shivering—long after you should have turned out the lights.

First up is the newest from Jane Toombs. *The Volan Curse* has it all: a sexy hero with just a touch of amnesia, and an innocent heroine who believes in the power of love and the hero's innocence—she hopes! There's also an evil family curse and a couple of villains who'll scare you out of your wits and make you glad you're safe at home, not roaming the grounds of Fenn Volan's familial estate.

Then travel back in time with Vivian Knight Jenkins in *By Love Possessed*. The post-Civil War past is only a lightning storm away for Liz Hayden. And so is a passionate affair with Garrett Rowland, the most sensual man she's ever met. But is he also the murderer history has branded him?

Next month, expect another shiveringly good time here at Shadows. And until then, be careful where you look for love. You never know what might be waiting for you ... in the dark.

Yours,

Leslie J. Wainger
Senior Editor and Editorial Coordinator

Please address questions and book requests to:
Reader Service
U.S.: P.O. Box 1325, Buffalo, NY 14269
Canadian: P.O. Box 1050, Niagara Falls, Ont. L2E 7G7

JANE TOOMBS

THE VOLAN Curse

Published by Silhouette Books
America's Publisher of Contemporary Romance

SILHOUETTE BOOKS

ISBN 0-373-27035-6

THE VOLAN CURSE

Copyright © 1994 by Jane Toombs

Books by Jane Toombs

Silhouette Shadows

JANE TOOMBS

believes that a touch of the mysterious adds spice to a romance. Her childhood fascination with stories about shape changers such as vampires, werewolves and shamans never faded, leading to her present interest in supernatural influences, not only in Gothic romances but in the early cultures of all peoples.

A Californian transplanted to New York, Jane and her writer husband live in the shadow of Storm King Mountain.

PROLOGUE

As soon as the elevator doors opened, Theodore Volan wheeled out and down the corridor with the air of a man who had every right to be on the sixth floor of the hospital. He'd discovered early in life how easy it was to bluff others, and now that he was in his seventies his skill was honed to perfection.

As he'd surmised, no one cast a second look at the well-dressed, handsome, graying man who, despite being wheelchair-bound, wore arrogance like a mantle. He ignored the ache in his shoulders as he sent the chair spinning onto the pediatric unit—damp weather was hell on arthritic joints, and California's far northern coast was rarely free of fog. In fact, fog caressed Eureka as fervently and frequently as the most ardent of lovers.

Theo smiled wryly at the fanciful notion. He'd been an ardent enough lover in his time—but no more.

White-clad nurses were clustered at the unit station. He'd timed his arrival for the change of shift in order to look over as many of them at once as he could. He was almost certain the one he needed worked on this unit.

He had to reach the station before they sequestered themselves for the change-of-shift report. The months of recovery after his accident two years ago and then subsequently being hospitalized for a heart attack had made him an expert on how things were run in this place.

He wheeled up to the station, quickly scanning each nurse. Not that one. Nor that one. No. No. No. None of them. Damn! He swung the chair around, disappointment slowing his movements. He'd been so sure he'd find the one he wanted here. Now what?

His train of thought unlinked abruptly as he became aware of the young woman in white hurrying along the corridor toward the unit. He'd never seen her before. Probably in her late twenties. Blond hair, trim figure, attractive. None of that counted; he didn't care what she looked like.

As she neared him, he gripped his cane in his gloved hands and thrust it in front of her to bar her way.

"You!" he exclaimed. "You're the one!"

CHAPTER ONE

Neita Metsula wished she'd left Eureka earlier. The gray September afternoon had already slid into dusk, and her compact car, not designed for long and steep hills, climbed slowly, its headlights probing the increasing gloom. The road had quickly narrowed to a bare two lanes, unmarked by any white or yellow lines, with trees crowding to the very edge of the blacktop on both sides. Arriving at Halfmoon House in the dark didn't appeal to her; she'd hoped to get a good look at the place before venturing inside.

She didn't know exactly what made her uneasy. Once she'd gotten over the abrupt and unorthodox way Mr. Volan had recruited her, she'd found him businesslike and courteous. As well as *very* generous.

She'd had no sense of darkness while talking to him—on the contrary, he was one of those rare few she thought of as sunshine people, those with an inner glow. Most people were neither dark nor light, but occasionally she met an exception like Theodore Volan. She'd had this odd ability to perceive hidden traits in a person since she was a child and, over time, she'd learned to avoid *shadowed* people.

She knew there was nothing to fear from a sunshine person, so why was she left with this nebulous worry that Mr. Volan expected something from her other than nursing? Nothing so blatant as sex—

something more secret and subtle. But what? Had she been too hasty in accepting the job as his thirty-four-year-old nephew's private-duty nurse?

Mr. Volan was paying her far more than she could possibly make at the hospital, and she'd be living at Halfmoon House, thus saving on room and board. Now, belatedly, she wondered if the pay was *too* generous.

He'd told her Halfmoon House was about fifteen miles north of Eureka, but what he'd neglected to say was that the last mile was all uphill. And "sits by itself" wasn't quite the same as totally isolated—except for the farm near the bottom of the hill, she hadn't passed any houses, for what seemed a very long time.

Perhaps the reason she found this wilderness daunting was because she'd spent most of her thirty years in the Bay Area where one city segued into another to create a mammoth metropolis. She'd arrived in Eureka only a month ago and hadn't yet gotten used to the smallness of the city. Now here she was, only a few miles away from Eureka and smack-dab in the middle of the woods.

Fenn Volan, she'd been told, was recuperating from injuries suffered in a serious accident; apparently he'd fallen from a cliff, though he had no memory of what had happened. A convalescent patient should present no problems for her—that is, if Mr. Volan had been honest about his nephew's condition. Selective amnesia following trauma was common enough, but what if Fenn suffered from a more serious mental illness, one his uncle either wouldn't admit to himself or had deliberately concealed from her?

Stop borrowing trouble, Neita ordered herself. It's more than likely you'll find Fenn Volan's condition exactly as described; if not, and your patient proves impossible, you can always leave.

Just as she was despairing over ever coming to the top of the hill, the road leveled and the trees thinned, giving way to ornamental bushes. At the same moment, the gibbous moon broke through the cloud cover, its rays trapping a tall, many-chimneyed house in a web of silver.

Lights glowed from the top of a central square tower thrusting above the chimneys. An old Victorian house, Neita told herself, probably of the style Californians called Barbary Coast gothic—she'd be able to tell better by daylight. There was absolutely nothing intimidating about the place, tower included. Or, at least, there wouldn't be if the house stood on a city street.

She drove around the circle and parked directly in front of the steps leading up to the archway sheltering the front door. As she started to get out of the car, an ululating howl, eerie and threatening, froze her in place. Hair rose on her nape and along her arms. She'd never heard such a frightening sound.

After a moment she pulled herself together. Judging that the howling beast couldn't be close enough to attack her, she leapt from the car, ran up the steps, grasped the iron knocker and banged it hard on the strike plate—once, twice, three times. As she listened nervously for a repeat of the howling, an eternity passed before the door swung open.

A stocky white-haired man wearing a suit and tie peered at her, blocking her entrance.

"I'm Neita Metsula," she told him, edging closer as she spoke, making him back away so she could ease into the safety of the house. "Mr. Theodore Volan hired me as his nephew's nurse."

"My name's Barnes, Ms. Metsula," he said, stepping aside and gesturing her into an arched-ceilinged foyer. "Mr. Theo's houseman."

"I didn't mean to push past you so rudely," she said, "but that howling outside made me rather nervous. What in the world was it?"

"Howling, Ms. Metsula?"

"Like a wolf's howl—surely you heard it."

Barnes shook his head. "There are no wolves in these parts. Or anywhere in California, I should think, except in zoos."

"I suppose it might have been a coyote," she said dubiously. "You did hear the howling, didn't you?"

"I'm afraid not. We do have Doberman guard dogs, but they rarely make any noise, and when they do, they bark, not howl. Now that you've arrived, I'll turn them loose for the night. If you'll follow me, Ms., I'll show you to your room, then fetch your bags."

Neita, unused to being waited on by servants, felt guilty as she trailed Barnes up a long curving staircase. If she hadn't been startled by the howling, she'd have brought her bags in with her.

Looking over the ornately carved walnut rail to the foyer below and breathing in a lemony scent that might have been polish, she told herself the entry was at least as large as the entire living room of her old apartment in San Francisco. Her glance slid along the furnishings, and she briefly noted the gleam of mellowed wood and rich fabrics before facing forward once more. If she stayed, tomorrow was soon enough to be impressed by Halfmoon House. Her patient came first.

"I'd like to see Mr. Fenn Volan as soon as possible," she told Barnes as they turned left at the head of the stairs and proceeded along a short corridor.

"I'll inform him you're here," Barnes said. "Since Mr. Theo announced you'd be with Mr. Fenn as much as possible, I've taken the liberty of giving you the room adjoining his."

"Adjoining? With a connecting door?"

"Yes, of course. Isn't it customary?"

Obviously it was logical for a nurse to be close to her patient, though Neita hadn't expected to be confronted with a connecting door. After all, Fenn Volan was convalescent, not seriously ill. She nodded uncertainly at Barnes, wishing she knew more about the protocol for live-in private-duty nurses. She might be a well trained, capable nurse but her experience had been only in hospitals.

Barnes ushered her into a charming room with pale blue walls and three windows that ran almost from floor to ceiling. Several chairs and small tables and a dresser in a recess complemented the muted color scheme. The bed was brass.

"What a lovely room," she said.

"The windows open onto a small balcony." Barnes gestured discreetly toward a door in the recess. "The bathroom. The other door is the one to Mr. Fenn's room." He inclined his head before departing.

Left alone, Neita checked her appearance in what was obviously an expensive antique mirror over the dresser and decided she looked as uncertain as she felt.

That would never do. She tucked a stray wisp of her blond hair into the neat twist at the back of her head, glanced into the bathroom, then pulled the lightweight curtains aside to look out. The moon had disappeared; she saw nothing but darkness.

Removing her jacket, she hung it in a small closet, closing the folding doors before turning to see Barnes carrying her two suitcases into the room.

"I've spoken to Mr. Fenn," he said. "Please knock at the connecting door when you're ready to see him." Once again he left her alone.

The door, like the other woodwork in the room, was painted a very pale gray that blended with the blue of the walls. There was no bolt or key. Slipping into her professional mode, she tapped against the gray panel.

"Come in," a man's voice called.

The glass knob felt cool under her fingers. As she pushed the door open she breathed in a faint scent of woodsmoke, so she wasn't surprised when she stepped into the large room and found it lit only by firelight. Fenn lounged on a small sofa near the hearth but sat up straight when she entered.

"*You're* the nurse?" He sounded incredulous.

What had he expected? "Yes," she said firmly. "And you must be the patient."

He rose, favoring his left leg, and limped toward her. "You're quite a change from Jethro."

He was taller than her five foot eight and not a heavily built man, though his shoulders were broad. He wasn't conventionally handsome but he had an arresting face, one women would look at twice. His thick, dark and wavy hair grew to a point in the·center of his forehead, something her superstitious maternal grandmother used to call a devil's peak.

"Never trust a person whose hair grows like that," Grandma Randazzo had warned. "It's the devil's mark, that's what it is."

Neita no longer believed wholeheartedly in the tales of her grandparents—from either side of the family. Theo Volan's gray hair also came to a widow's peak, so the trait must run in the Volan family. While she was wondering if the trait was dominant or recessive, Fenn, his green eyes gazing into hers, grasped her hand in greeting. She stopped thinking. Stopped breathing. Her heart seemed to lurch, then speed into overdrive.

He blinked, and she had the impression of a sudden flare of light before he dropped her hand and stepped back, staring at her.

She knew he'd felt the power that leapt between them; nothing remotely like it had ever happened to her before. It was far more than sexual awareness, though that had been mixed in. As she fought to regain her professional cool, she strained for a sense of light or darkness but found neither.

"Who the hell are you?" he demanded, frowning.

"My name's Neita Metsula. I'm your nurse." She marveled at how calm she sounded when she was as shaken as he looked to be.

"Neita," he repeated. "Neita."

"It's a Finnish name, like Metsula," she said, growing nervous under his continued stare.

"Is that why your eyes tilt up at the far corners?" he asked, then shook his head. "Never mind. Shall we sit down?"

Quickly she chose a chair, avoiding the couch for fear he might sit next to her. He reseated himself on the couch. "First of all, I don't need a nurse," he said.

"Your uncle evidently believes otherwise or he wouldn't have hired me."

He went on as though she hadn't spoken. "And if I must have one, I prefer a man, like Jethro."

"Then you should have kept Jethro on," she snapped, losing patience with him.

"I would have if he hadn't disappeared. Zap—just like that. As though he'd vanished from the face of the earth."

His uncle had mentioned that Fenn's former nurse had left but he'd said nothing about a disappearance. She had no way of knowing if Fenn was imagining things or if his uncle had skirted around the truth.

"To be honest," she informed him, "I'm not entirely certain I wish to stay."

He straightened. "Why not?"

"You've just said you don't want me here."

"Ignore what I said for the moment. What's your other reason? Or reasons?"

Unwilling to admit she feared she'd been lied to about his mental stability or that she'd been badly shaken by the strange current that had leapt between them, Neita cast about for something to say but found nothing valid.

"This house is so isolated," she said finally, unable to come up with anything else. "And something really startled me when I arrived." Feeling a bit foolish about it now, she backtracked. "Maybe I overreacted."

"What startled you?" he asked.

She shrugged, turning both her hands palms upward. "I thought I heard some kind of an animal howling."

Fenn, who'd been leaning toward her, stared at her hands and recoiled as though she'd struck him. Without a word, he sprang to his feet and limped to the windows, pushing open the curtains to gaze into the night.

She rose and approached him hesitantly, noting with alarm the shudders rippling through his body.

"Fenn," she said softly. "Fenn, won't you tell me what's wrong?"

He didn't reply or respond in any way.

Neita bit her lip, fervently wishing she knew what had upset him. She glanced at her hands. He'd been staring at them as though something was wrong with them, but, of course, nothing was. Was he troubled because she'd mentioned the howling? Perhaps he'd heard it, too, even though Barnes claimed not to have.

Without knowing more about him, she didn't think it was wise to ask. What was the best course to follow? The fire crackled, flaring up momentarily, and she thought she saw an answering glow from Fenn, but it was gone before she could be positive. Somewhat reassured by this evidence of light, she edged closer.

In her experience, she'd noticed the laying on of hands often helped troubled patients, and so, keeping her voice low and even, she said, "Fenn, I'm going to put my hand on your shoulder." Very slowly and carefully she touched him, poised to leap away if he reacted violently.

This time she felt no shock. Apparently he didn't either because, though his shoulder quivered under her fingers, he gave no other indication he knew she was there. Using both hands, she began to stroke his shoulders, keeping her touch gentle but firm, aware hesitancy was not reassuring to someone in an agitated state.

"I'm here to help you," she said. This time her words got through.

"No one can help me!" Whirling, he glared down at her. "If you knew what was best for you, you'd get in your car and return to Eureka."

His sudden movement had surprised her into taking a step backward, but she felt no real fear of him. "Since you know nothing about me," she said evenly, "you have no idea whether I can help you or not."

Fenn turned to draw the curtains shut again, then limped to the couch, easing his left leg up onto it. "I don't think I'm crazy," he said, "but it's hell not to remember what happened to me."

She recognized this as a skewed apology for the way he'd behaved. At the same time, she realized she'd made up her mind he wasn't mentally ill. Distraught, yes, but within the realm of sanity. She wasn't certain she could help him but she intended to remain at Halfmoon House and try.

Standing beside the couch, she said, "I'll be in the adjoining room. If you need me during the night, call or tap on the door."

He half smiled. "Will you sleep well knowing there's no key to that connecting door?"

Annoyed, because she knew perfectly well how poorly she'd sleep, Neita replied tartly, "I'm quite certain you won't rape me, if that's what you mean."

His smile faded. "Don't be too sure of anything here at Halfmoon House, including me."

After leaving Fenn, Neita went in search of her employer, only to be told by Barnes that Mr. Theo had taken the lift up to the tower and was not to be disturbed.

A tall, raffishly good-looking blond man sauntered into the foyer while she was talking to Barnes. "Don't tell me you're the new nurse?" he said. At her nod, he smiled. "Quite an improvement over the last, don't you think, Barnes?"

"I'm Neita Metsula," she said, wondering who he was. Her employer hadn't mentioned others living in the house.

"I'm Fenn's cousin, Weslin," he said. "My sister and I dropped in for a visit, only to find Uncle Theo incommunicado and our cuz barricaded in his room. I don't think he's left it since he came home from the hospital. What a bonus you are. Do come and join me." He glanced at Barnes. "You might bring coffee and whatever goodies Emily can scare up into the living room."

When Neita hesitated, Weslin took her arm, urging her across the foyer, saying, "Please don't deny me the pleasure of your company. I'm really quite harmless."

Amused and disposed to like him, she said, "I think that's the line Little Red Riding Hood fell for."

Some emotion she couldn't quite identify gleamed in his amber eyes for a moment, then he laughed. "I can see this visit of mine will be more interesting than most."

The glowing colors of the Oriental rugs on the parquet floor of the living room brightened the dark walnut wall paneling. The golds, blues, whites and greens of the upholstered furniture further lightened the ambience. If the room hadn't been so large, Neita would have called it cozy.

Weslin stopped beside a conversational grouping of sofa and chairs, inviting her to be seated.

"You'll find Emily's an excellent cook," he said. "Uncle Theo hires only the best."

Since Theo Volan had hired her, there was no easy response to his comment. "Will your sister be joining us?" she asked, noticing with interest that Weslin, too, had a widow's peak, though less pronounced than Fenn's.

"Lycia? No, she's gone off to look for amusement elsewhere, and I doubt she'll be back until after midnight." A tinge of annoyance colored his words.

Barnes returned remarkably quickly with a serving cart laden with food. On his heels came Theo Volan in his wheelchair. Barnes left the cart by the table in front of the sofa and went out.

Theo nodded at Neita, his attention focused on his nephew. "I didn't expect to see you, Weslin. Are you alone?"

"Only temporarily. Lycia's with me."

For a moment Neita got the impression that Theo wasn't particularly pleased with the news, but then he smiled and she decided she'd been mistaken.

"You're always welcome here," Theo told Weslin. "I see you've met Ms. Metsula."

"A great improvement over Jethro, as I told her," Weslin said. "But I was under the impression Fenn didn't really need a nurse any longer."

"In my opinion, he still does."

Weslin shrugged. "I wouldn't dare to contradict you."

The edge of mockery in his voice made Neita uncomfortable and she started to rise, thinking perhaps the two men wished to be alone.

"No, no, please don't go," Theo said. "It would be a shame for you to miss Emily's famous blackberry cobbler. Would you mind doing the honors?" He gestured toward the cart and she saw he wore gloves, which was not unusual for a person using a wheelchair.

"I'll be glad to," she said, moving to the cart where she began dispensing food and drink. Somewhat to her surprise, Theo refused both. For a few moments no one spoke. After two forkfuls of the cobbler, Neita was about to make a remark about melts-in-yourmouth good when Theo turned to her.

"I raised the three of them, you know, Neita—Fenn and the twins, Lycia and Weslin," he said. "They're all the family I have." His voice was flat rather than emotional, and maybe that was why she felt the words hung in the air, almost, she thought, as though he'd uttered a warning. To her? To Weslin? But that didn't make sense; she was being foolish.

She feared her nod wasn't quite the right response, but she found no appropriate words.

"That's why Fenn's health is so important to me," Theo added.

"He always was your favorite." Though Weslin spoke wryly, there was an undercurrent of quite another emotion. Petulance? Disappointment?

Theo sighed. "I never have played favorites, though it's true I made extra time for Fenn. After the accident, you and Lycia had one another to cling to for consolation, but he had nobody except me."

"And now Fenn has a beautiful nurse to soothe his aches and pains," Weslin said lightly. "While Lycia deserts me for the bright lights of Eureka."

Neita felt that although one could never be sure what went on in an unfamiliar town, Eureka seemed to offer little in the way of exciting nightlife. She wondered about the accident Theo spoke of. Not Fenn's, obviously, but a much earlier accident, after which Theo had been left with three children to raise.

"I'd best return to my patient," she said, setting down her coffee cup and rising.

"You've met Fenn?" Theo asked her.

"Briefly." Weslin's presence inhibited her, keeping back the questions she wanted to ask her employer. No doubt there'd be time enough tomorrow. "Good night, then."

In her room, she resisted the impulse to look in on Fenn, feeling he might find it an intrusion. She satisfied her sense of duty by easing the door slightly ajar and calling softly, "If you need me, I'll be in my room for the rest of the night." Receiving no response, she left the door ajar and got ready for bed, cracking open one of the long windows to let in fresh air.

Neita hadn't expected to fall asleep easily—it was difficult to recall the last time she had. During the day she could hold the hounds of memory at bay, but once she crawled into bed they broke loose. Knowing it was useless, though, didn't prevent her from trying to control them.

You won't lose this patient, she assured herself. Fenn Volan is convalescent. He's all but well and he's not shadowed. While he may have a few problems, he's in no danger of dying. No danger at all.

In no way did Fenn's case resemble Patrick's. For one thing, Patrick had been only eighteen when he died. She took a deep breath, not wanting to bring back how hideously Patrick had died. Or how he'd almost taken her with him.

She'd made a terrible mistake when she tried to help Patrick. The appearance of the shadow should have warned her, but she hadn't paid close enough attention or she wouldn't have persisted. She doubted if anyone could help shadowed people.

Maybe what finally happened *was,* as Patrick had claimed on that last, ghastly night, her fault. Perhaps if she'd left him alone, he'd still be alive. And she'd still be whole....

Neita curled into a ball, fists clenched as she struggled not to relive the past. She'd almost given up the useless battle when a faint, far-off sound brought her upright in bed, listening, the hair prickling along her arms.

From beyond her windows, out in the darkness of the night, something howled.

CHAPTER TWO

The howling wasn't repeated. Telling herself it must be a coyote, and in any case she was safe inside, Neita eventually slipped into sleep. She woke to muffled cries, finding herself disoriented for a moment in the darkness. Once she was fully awake, she realized the sound was coming from next door, from her patient. Leaping from the bed, she grabbed her robe and hurried through the connecting door into Fenn's room.

Only red embers remained in the fireplace. In the moonlight streaming through the open curtains onto his bed, she saw Fenn thrashing and struggling as though fighting off invisible enemies. Knowing better than to touch him when he was trapped in a nightmare, she stood at the foot of his mahogany four-poster.

"Fenn," she said, in as normal and calm a tone as she could. "Wake up. Now."

He sat up abruptly, his eyes open and staring toward her. "No," he whispered. "No, don't come any closer."

It took her a moment to realize he was not awake but in a somnambulistic state where he didn't really see her. "I'm Neita Metsula, your nurse," she told him, speaking more sharply than before. "Wake up, Fenn."

"I won't," he muttered. "You can't make me."

Difficult as it was to believe he wasn't responding to what she said, his blank stare convinced her that he was still caught between sleeping and waking, still in an alternate state of consciousness—the textbooks called it dissociative phenomena. Like amnesia.

Abandoning her attempt to rouse him—it was likely to be ineffectual, anyway—she watched and listened, remembering more about sleepwalking. In this state, adults often acted out what was troubling them. Perhaps she'd find clues from what he did and said that might help him recover his lost memories.

Still sitting, Fenn edged sideways, inching closer and closer to the edge. "Stay away from me!" he cried suddenly and flung himself to the side. Before she could move, he slid off the bed and sprawled onto the floor.

By the time she reached him, he was sitting up, cursing under his breath. "Are you awake, Fenn?" she asked.

He started at her voice, turning to look at her. "Neita!" He got to his feet. "I must have fallen out of bed again."

"Again?" she echoed. "How often does it happen?"

He stood in front of her with the moon bright on his face, lighting his forehead and high cheekbones while shadows darkened the rest of his features, creating a demonic mask, making him appear menacing and sinister. She resisted the impulse to take a step backward, telling herself firmly that his shadows were on the outside; she sensed no darkness from within him.

"It happens now and then. When the moon—" He broke off, turning toward the source of the silver light, then back to her. "I know I closed the curtains. Did you open them?"

"No. I didn't enter your room until a few minutes ago, when I heard you thrashing around."

"Someone did. I *know* I shut them." As he spoke he crossed to the window and yanked the curtains together, shutting out the moonlight and plunging the room into darkness. "I'll be all right now. Go back to bed, Neita."

She didn't see what more she could do for him and, to tell the truth, being alone in the dark with him unnerved her a bit. What should she believe about the curtains? That he hadn't closed them, that he'd risen in his sleep and opened them, or that someone had actually entered his room and opened his closed curtains? At this point, she didn't know Fenn or anyone else in the house well enough to decide what the truth might be.

Guided by the faint light shining from her open door—the curtains in her own room weren't drawn—she started to leave him. At the connecting door she paused, reminded of what she'd heard before she'd dropped off to sleep.

"Are there coyotes around here?" she asked.

"Probably." He clipped the word short.

Her hand on the door, she hesitated, words from an old blessing of her Finnish grandmother circling in her head: *Luonotar oi Ilman Neiti*—Luonotar, Lady of Creation, watch over this one for my sake....

It was a prayer for another; Grandmother Metsula had always asked Luonotar to watch over little Neita and keep her safe.

Why does such a blessing occur to me now? Neita asked herself. Is it Fenn I feel needs Luonotar's protection? Or do I? And why am I thinking of Luonotar, anyway? I gave up that nonsense years ago.

Shaking her head, she called, "Good night," and left Fenn's room, shutting the door firmly behind her. A moment later, she eased it ajar again. He was, after all, her patient and he might need her.

It didn't occur to her until she was once more under her covers that Fenn's falling out of bed while in a somnambulistic state might be a reenactment of the accident he didn't consciously remember. According to his uncle, Fenn had been found unconscious and badly injured by a forest ranger at the foot of a cliff in the nearby mountains.

If he'd been reliving the accident, then what he'd said while in this altered state might be significant. *Stay away from me!* he'd cried. What had menaced him? An animal? Or worse, a person? Had this unknown menace driven him over the edge of the cliff?

Neita sighed. Likely enough she was reading too much into one sleepwalking episode. Still, she didn't intend to dismiss it entirely. And when she felt discussing it wouldn't disturb Fenn too much, she meant to bring up the possible connection between the somnambulism and his amnesia.

Her last thought before she slipped into sleep's dark embrace was that if she meant to keep her relationship with Fenn strictly professional, she'd have to forget the powerful surge of awareness that sprang to life at their first touch, an awareness still lingering in both her mind and her body....

* * *

Fenn sat propped up on his bed, staring into the darkness. There had *not* been anything on the palm of Neita's right hand, he told himself. Nothing. He'd hallucinated the five-pointed star within a circle. He knew the red pentagram had been a momentary hallucination because when he'd looked again, the sinister symbol was gone.

A shudder ran through him as a childhood memory surfaced. Amnesia was one hell of a tricky thing, taking away memories you needed and allowing you to keep those you'd rather forget.

He hadn't thought about Aunt Hensa, the twins' mother, for years and he didn't care to think of her now, but her low, throaty voice echoed in his ears as an image of amber eyes set aslant in her thin face formed in his mind.

"Look, look, what's this I see on your palm?" she'd asked his friend Donny.

It was a rainy Saturday. He and Donny, both five, had been playing with his toy soldiers in the Volan attic. Neither of them had heard Aunt Hensa come up the stairs.

"I don't see nothing," Donny said, while little Fenn looked on, wishing his aunt would go away. You were supposed to like all your relatives but he didn't like Hensa. In fact, he was kind of scared of her.

"See," Aunt Hensa said, holding Donny's right hand while she traced a pattern on his palm with one long red fingernail. "Here's the circle, red as blood, and here's the star inside that circle."

"I still can't see it," Donny told her, looking from his hand to her face, staring into Hensa's glowing yellow eyes.

"See the pentagram or not, my sweet, you can't escape." Aunt Hensa had smiled and hugged Donny then and kissed him right on the mouth. Fenn would have hated it, but Donny didn't seem to mind. He even seemed to like being kissed.

Fenn had never forgotten the incident. How could he after what had happened later?

He sprang from the bed, shaking his head as if the movement could rid him of those terrible childhood memories. Padding to the connecting door, he eased it open wider and looked into Neita's room. Her curtains were open and the moon shone in, its silver light illuminating her closed eyes and the fair hair spread over her pillow.

For a moment he imagined himself next to her, running his fingers through the silk of her hair, then bringing his hands down to cup her face before he kissed those slightly parted lips....

Damn! Fenn turned abruptly away from the door and limped back into the darkness of his room. Why in hell had Uncle Theo hired a female nurse, anyway? Why bring a defenseless young woman here? And worse, an attractive woman, one he found himself drawn to against his will. He hadn't forgotten the jolt when he'd first touched her, a compulsion so powerful and compelling he'd damned near pulled her into his arms then and there.

Even if he dared to indulge himself—assuming she was willing—he couldn't afford the distraction of an affair. It was far too dangerous. For both of them. His desperate need to recover his lost memory came first. And if he did recover it, what then?

Fenn grimaced in despair. Amnesia might conceal what had occurred before his accident, but in his heart he knew something dreadful had happened. He doubted, though, that it could be any worse than what he feared had taken place. Danger surrounded him. Or perhaps it would be more accurate to say danger arose from him.

What howled under the moon? He'd heard the howling before, on the same night Jethro had vanished. He'd thought of the howling as a summons to him, fearing he alone could hear it. If so, it couldn't be real.

He would have asked Uncle Theo but his uncle seemed reluctant to talk to him since the accident—almost afraid. Theo's recent heart attack had changed his uncle in ways that confused Fenn. For this reason he'd hesitated to mention the howling to Uncle Theo, though he *had* intended to ask Jethro if he'd heard it. But Jethro had never returned. Scared off? His disappearance left Fenn uneasy.

And now, tonight, the howling had come again. But since Neita had heard it, he knew for certain something was out there under the moon. She'd asked about coyotes, but no coyote made that deep-throated haunting cry—and wolves no longer roamed the hills of California.

First the eerie howling, then the damn pentagram. Hallucination or not, he worried about his vision of the star within a circle because tradition gave that symbol an ominous meaning. When the pentagram marked a palm, the sign foretold who was to be next—

if he believed in such things. Before his accident he might have laughed off the warning, but with his memory of that time gone and with the all-too-real nightmares plaguing him, he no longer could afford to scoff at mythic symbols.

Neita was here in his uncle's house. She was sleeping in the room next to his, rooms connected by an unlocked door, unaware she'd already been marked as a victim. His victim? He clenched his jaw. God, if only he could penetrate the thick fog of amnesia that hid the truth.

One thing seemed clear. If she wasn't here, how could Neita be a victim? Whether he believed in the pentagram or not, he didn't dare take chances, so tomorrow he'd convince Uncle Theo to send her away. He didn't need a nurse. Why did his uncle persist in saying he did?

Unless Theo was hiding something from him. What kind of a nurse was she? Psychiatric?

She wasn't anything like Jethro, and it was more than the difference of male and female. She touched some chord in him that no other person had ever found.

As if drawn by invisible strings, he rose and approached the connecting door again, this time entering Neita's room, moving quietly to the edge of her bed. Silver light no longer streamed in; the moon was edging down the night sky, preparing to set. Yet there was enough illumination for him to see her.

Reaching out, he touched her hair where it lay on the pillow. The silken strand clung to his fingers as he drew back his hand, seeming to urge him not to go.

Are you here because my uncle believes I've lost my reason along with some of my memories? he asked silently. Have you come to watch my every action, evaluate my every mood? Does Uncle Theo expect you to be able to save me?

The last two words echoed over and over in his head—*save me, save me, save me....*

He sighed and was about to turn away when Neita sat up so abruptly she startled him into taking a step backward. She slid one hand under her pillow.

"What do you want? Are you in pain?" Reasonable as her words were, he heard a betraying quiver of fear in her voice.

He meant to apologize for frightening her, but instead he heard himself saying, "Do they think I'm losing my mind? Is that why you're here?"

She studied him for long moments, then drew her hand from under the pillow. There was nothing in it. "Amnesia is not madness," she said, crossing her legs Indian-fashion under the covers and arranging herself more comfortably. "Do you routinely skulk in your room?"

The sudden question took him by surprise and also annoyed him. "I deny skulking," he said. "It so happens I prefer to be by myself."

"You may as well sit down while we talk," she said.

Knowing he ought to leave, he found himself pulling a small rocker up near the bed and seating himself. "I came in here on impulse," he told her.

"Let's start off by being truthful," she suggested. "You came in here because you needed something. A listener?"

Without answering, he reverted to her first question. "I do *not* skulk."

"How far can you walk without pain?"

"Do you always try to keep your patients off-balance?" he demanded.

"When were you last outdoors?"

He raised his eyebrows. "I've heard of tough nurses, but you had me fooled because you sure as hell don't look like one. I'll answer your questions if you'll answer mine—is it a bargain?" After her nod, he said, "I think I'd be able to walk about a half mile, using my cane. I haven't attempted it because, in case you haven't noticed, we've had quite a bit of rain lately." He paused and shook his head. "You said be honest. Okay, I'll give it a shot. I don't want to go outside—I'm not sure why."

"We'll try taking a walk tomorrow, rain or shine. In answer to your questions, I'm here because your uncle insisted you needed a nurse and, for some reason, decided I was the only one who would do. Amnesia is very disturbing to anyone's peace of mind because, in a sense, memories are what we are, each and every one of us. Losing a memory is losing part of yourself."

But what if you're afraid to regain the part of yourself that's lost? he thought but didn't say.

"I was going to wait until we were better acquainted to bring this up," she continued, "but I've changed my mind. You ought to hear it right away. When you fell out of your bed while you were sleepwalking, I wondered if you were, in your somnambulistic state, reenacting the accident you had. People do this, you know."

He hadn't known. Could she possibly be right?

"You were also talking," she added, and went on to tell him what he'd said.

He stared at her, recalling fragments of his nightmares, shards of horror that fit in with what she'd heard him say. "Jethro never mentioned sleepwalking," he said at last. "Nor talking."

They sat in silence for some time, Fenn sunk in thought, until he realized he was undoubtedly overstaying his welcome. A somewhat reluctant welcome, but, considering the circumstances, he didn't blame her.

He rose from the rocker. "What I really came in here for was to touch you," he admitted. He heard her draw in her breath, but she didn't speak. "Your hair was spread over the pillow and I did touch it." Recalling how a strand of her hair had clung to his fingers, he smiled. "Actually, I was about to return to my room when you woke."

"I'm a light sleeper."

"I'm duly warned."

"If you do need me in the night, all you have to do is call my name and I'll come to you," she said.

"My dear Ms. Metsula, that's an open-ended invitation if ever I heard one."

She bit her lip, but he had the feeling it was to suppress a smile. "You know how I meant it, Mr. Volan," she countered.

"Do I?" Two steps brought him to her bedside. Before she could move, he bent and slid his hand under her pillow. When he pulled it out he was holding a small silver dagger with a sharply pointed two-edged blade.

"So much for trusting your patients," he said, handing her back the knife.

"I find trust much easier when carrying my grandmother's dagger," she said coolly.

He grasped her free hand and brought it to his lips, kissing the unblemished palm. "I'll rest easier knowing you're armed," he told her as he dropped her hand. "Good night, Neita."

As he turned and strode from her room, he realized he no longer wanted her to leave. She made him angry and annoyed, true. But this was the first time since the accident that he'd also felt fully alive.

CHAPTER THREE

Despite her disturbed night, Neita woke at her accustomed early hour. She showered and, since there was no reason to wear a uniform, put on a white shirt, blue denim skirt and a pair of low-heeled sandals. She glanced in at Fenn. Seeing him sprawled on his stomach, asleep on top of his covers, she quietly shut the connecting door and left her room.

Downstairs, Barnes seemed a bit surprised to see her. "No one in the family gets up early," he told her. "Mr. Theo takes his breakfast on a tray in his room and so does Mr. Fenn."

Deciding to wait another day before insisting Fenn come out of his room to eat, Neita simply nodded. "What about Weslin and his sister?"

"They usually eat in the morning room, but I doubt if we'll see them much before noon."

"Do you think the cook—Emily, is it?—would mind if I had my breakfast in the kitchen this morning?" Neita asked.

Barnes's smile was a bit stiff but it *was* a smile. "Emily would be pleased."

The cook was a plump, freckle-faced woman of about forty with prominent blue eyes and orange-red hair. "Pleased to meet you," she told Neita. "Sure, take a seat here at the table and I'll fix whatever you want."

Quelling the impulse to insist she could serve herself—it was Emily's kitchen, not hers—Neita said, "I need a cup of black coffee in the morning before I can really begin to function. In a mug, if you don't mind."

Setting the mug of coffee in front of her, Emily said, "Seeing as how you didn't ask for decaf, I guess you're not one of them health-food people. Thought you might be since you're a nurse."

"I try to eat healthy, but I don't go overboard. I think I'll risk an egg this morning—scrambled."

When she finished the egg, plus the two pieces of toasted homemade bread Emily gave her, Neita said, "I knew you were a great cook as soon as I took the first bite of your cobbler last night."

Emily smiled. "That male nurse, Jethro, was partial to my cobblers, too." Her smile faded and she shook her head. "I can't imagine whatever could've happened to him. He didn't seem like the sort who'd go running off without a word to anyone."

Unease prickled the hair on Neita's nape. So Jethro hadn't simply quit his job. Fenn had been right when he said Jethro had vanished.

"Just a month ago, it was," Emily went on. "Mr. Theo's been looking for another nurse ever since. He can be a very particular man, Mr. Theo can, and he couldn't seem to find whatever it was he wanted in a nurse. Not till he came across you."

"Fenn's been without a nurse for a month?" Neita's amazement showed in her voice. No one had told her. If he'd gotten by for that long on his own, no wonder Fenn had insisted he didn't need a nurse.

Emily nodded but didn't comment further. "Like a refill on that coffee?" Without waiting for a yes or no, she poured Neita another mugful and then took down a mug for herself. "I believe I'll join you. Coffee does pep me up something wonderful."

She settled into a chair across the table from Neita. "I guess you met the twins," she said. "We haven't seen them since last month. They've been coming here more often since Mr. Fenn's accident—before that it might be six to eight months between their visits."

"I met Weslin but not his sister."

"They don't look nothing alike. You'd swear Miss Lycia and Mr. Fenn were the twins instead. 'Course, they *are* cousins. The three of them are children of Mr. Theo's two brothers." Emily sighed. "Burned to death in a fire, his bothers did, along with their wives. 'Twas nothing less than a miracle the children weren't there when it happened. I suppose you know Mr. Theo raised all of them."

Neita nodded, thinking the tragedy must have been devastating for Theo as well as the twins and Fenn.

"They were teenagers when I came to work here," Emily said. "Seems like old times having Mr. Fenn staying at the house again."

"What kind of a boy was he?"

"They were all smart kids, Mr. Fenn maybe the brightest. He was good-hearted, too. Not to say the twins weren't, but they always thought of each other first—I guess that's normal for twins. I must say, Miss Lycia got to be a real handful before she went off to college. The boys got in a scrape or two, like boys do, but she was something else again." Emily shook her head. "Still, she did have a way of getting around you that made you forgive her no matter what."

Emily took a long swallow of coffee, put down her mug and looked at Neita. "You're asking me about Mr. Fenn on account of how he won't come out of his room, aren't you? All I can say is he wasn't like that before the accident. I told Barnes it must be he got his brain concussed, like you hear about, to make him change the way he has."

"It takes time to recover after any accident," Neita said. She finished her coffee and rose. "Thanks for the breakfast."

"Wasn't no bother. I like a bit of company."

Neita returned to her room. When she eased the connecting door open to check on Fenn, she was startled to see an attractive dark-haired woman lounging on his bed in the sheerest of robes. Lycia, she decided. Fenn was nowhere in sight, but Neita could hear his shower running.

Though Neita hadn't made a sound, Lycia turned to look at her. "You must be the new nurse," she drawled in a low, throaty voice. "How strange Uncle Theo chose a woman, knowing that—" She paused as the water stopped running and glanced at Fenn's closed bathroom door. "Wes told me your name but I've forgotten."

"Neita Metsula."

What had Lycia been about to tell her? Neita wondered, watching Fenn's cousin yawn and stretch. The revealing robe clearly showed her lissome figure. Lycia did resemble Fenn except for her eyes, yellow like her twin's. She was certainly a striking woman, her dark hair sweeping back from the Volan widow's peak. Though Neita sensed no darkness around Lycia, something about her was disturbing.

Lycia sat up and smiled lazily. "Fenn won't be needing you for the next hour or so—I'll be keeping him company."

Neita didn't move. "I'm sure he'll enjoy seeing you."

Lycia lifted one perfectly arched brow. "There's no need to play supernurse, Neita. I'm perfectly safe with Cousin Fenn."

And just what am I supposed to read into that? Neita wondered. That Fenn can be dangerous? That I'm overstepping my boundaries? Or both? It's obvious she wants to be alone with him.

Though Neita couldn't see what harm it would do to leave the two of them alone, stubbornness kept her standing in the doorway. Lycia wasn't her employer and she had no intention of taking orders from her.

"Must I spell it out for you?" Lycia asked.

Suppressing a twinge of annoyance, Neita tried to smile pleasantly but she wasn't too sure she succeeded. "I'll just wait for my patient, if you don't mind."

"If the both of you don't mind," Fenn said, his voice startling Neita since she hadn't heard his bathroom door open, "I wish you'd get the hell out of my room so I can dress."

He wore nothing but a towel, his dark hair damp from the shower. The equally dark hair on his chest veed down to disappear under the towel. Lycia seemed as mesmerized by his lean masculinity as Neita was. Except for recent, still pink scars on his left leg, nothing marred his perfection.

"Now!" he growled, scowling from one to the other of them.

Lycia rose from his bed, swayed over to Fenn and reached up to kiss him. He turned his face so her mouth grazed his cheek. She shrugged and walked on to the door where she paused and murmured, "Later, dear cuz," before letting herself out.

"Please let me know when you're dressed," Neita said to Fenn. She stepped back into her room and closed the connecting door.

Crossing to the window, she looked down at the grounds below, seeing a green sweep of lawn ending in a high cypress hedge. Beyond the hedge, tall evergreens rose. But her mind wasn't on the view. Why, she wondered, had she resisted leaving Lycia alone with Fenn? Because she certainly had. Lycia and Fenn had grown up together, they were cousins—she was the stranger, the interloper. And yet she'd felt compelled to interfere.

Had she been trying to protect her patient? From what? It seemed obvious from his dismissal of them both that Fenn was quite capable of dealing with Lycia.

Certainly it's not jealousy on my part, Neita told herself. That would be ridiculous. Quite likely it meant nothing that Lycia had been lying on Fenn's bed in such a revealing robe—they'd been raised together, after all.

In any case, it was none of her business. The last thing she wanted was a relationship with Fenn other than nurse and patient.

Barnes appeared on the lawn below with two Dobermans on leashes, the big dogs tugging him along as they followed a scent trail toward the cypress hedge. Dobermans don't howl, Barnes had said. She had no reason to suspect he wasn't telling the truth, so it wasn't either of the dogs she'd heard in the night.

Coyotes, she told herself firmly. Coyotes singing to the moon, as a Miwok friend of hers had once said. But Neita couldn't make herself believe she'd listened to coyotes. She'd heard only one beast, and it had not, by any stretch of the imagination, been singing. She'd have described it as a chilling howl, unspeakably threatening.

Hear me and be warned.

Where were these morbid thoughts coming from? Neita asked herself. She refused to slip back into the slough of depression that had plagued her while she was recovering from the injuries she suffered when Patrick died. She'd put that awful time behind her when she left the Bay Area. Eureka was meant to be a new start, a new life.

Unwillingly caught in the past, a past she didn't want to remember, she jumped when Fenn tapped on the connecting door. "I'm ready," he called.

When she opened the door, he was standing there scowling. "I don't need a nurse hovering over me," he growled. "I told you that last night."

"I didn't mean to interfere in family matters this morning—" she began before he cut her off with an abrupt wave of his hand.

"This morning has nothing to do with it. The fact is, I'm perfectly capable of taking care of myself. I've been doing it since Jethro—"

"You're wrong," she said sharply. "You may have recovered physically, but psychically you haven't healed. Or you wouldn't hole up in this room."

His eyes narrowed. "I prefer keeping to myself."

"You've done that long enough."

"What the devil do you mean?"

"The sun's shining, it's a beautiful day. I thought we'd have lunch alfresco—a picnic on the grounds." She hadn't planned any such thing until this moment. Staring into his green gaze, she said, "I realize this amounts to a challenge for you."

Watching his jaw muscles clench, she feared she'd pushed him too far too soon and that he'd refuse.

After long moments he muttered, "Why not?" His lips twisted into a wry smile as he added, "I can't remember when I last went on a picnic."

Thinking it was a good sign that he could joke about his amnesia, she smiled back at him, pleased that her spur-of-the-moment ploy had worked. "I'll go down and ask Emily to make sandwiches and whatever," she said.

"We'll go down," he corrected. "It's past time I stopped making Emily carry trays up and down the stairs."

Elated at her unexpected success, she waited for him to retrieve his cane, not fetching it herself lest she be accused of "hovering." He didn't hesitate, as she'd thought he might do before stepping into the hall, but she noticed he was gripping the cane handle so tightly that his knuckles were white.

Fenn eyed the door enclosing Uncle Theo's lift that ran from the first floor to the tower, then turned toward the long, curving staircase to the foyer, determined to prove to Neita that he was in no sense an invalid.

The steps took a bit of managing, but he descended them slowly, arriving at the bottom without any real problem. Navigating the staircase had momentarily taken his attention away from the fact that he was no longer safe in his own room. When he realized what he was thinking, Fenn blinked.

Safe in his own room? What the hell was going on in his mind? What was there to be afraid of in Uncle Theo's house? Or outside the house, for that matter?

A darkness seemed to blur his vision, making him stop abruptly while he dealt with the demon from within that insisted, *You're not safe anywhere.*

He shuddered, starting when a hand touched his arm.

"Rest a moment if you're tired," Neita said.

The sound of her voice cleared his vision and chased the dark thought from his mind. "I'm fine," he said gruffly. But he knew he hadn't been, not until she touched him and made him aware he wasn't alone.

You might not need a nurse, he told himself, but apparently you do need Neita.

In the kitchen, Emily made a great fuss over serving him breakfast. While he ate, Neita talked to her about the picnic. Emily unearthed a large wicker basket that Fenn vaguely recalled from earlier days, and the two women were in the midst of planning what to bring along when Weslin strolled into the room.

"So the convalescent is abroad at last," he said, clapping Fenn on the back. "Good to see you up and about, cuz."

Emily bustled over to ask what Weslin wanted to eat, and he wound up sharing the table with Fenn.

"That looks like our old picnic basket," Weslin remarked. "Am I missing out on something?"

Did he want his cousins along on the picnic? Fenn wondered. Somehow he'd grown apart from Weslin in the past few years and he'd consciously avoided being alone with Lycia. Still, the shared memories of childhood provided an unbreakable bond. Except for Uncle Theo, the twins were his only relatives; the same blood ran in their veins. Besides, having people he knew and trusted with him when he left the house might help keep that blasted demon of panic from resurfacing.

"Neita's planned a picnic for my first outing," he told Weslin. "Why don't you and Lycia join us?"

"How could anyone refuse a combination of the great outdoors and Emily's food?" Weslin said. "And, of course, delightful company." He smiled at Neita before turning back to Fenn. "She's a refreshing change from hulking Jethro, don't you find?"

"There's no comparison," Fenn admitted. He'd appreciated the strong arm of his male nurse when he first was released from the hospital, but there was no denying Jethro had stressed physical improvement while ignoring all else. Neita, on the other hand, had immediately forced him from his lair. She'd also unsettled and confused him.

"Where and when is the picnic?" Weslin asked.

"We'll meet you and Lycia in the gazebo at three," Fenn told him, rising.

Weslin raised his eyebrows. "Back to your room so soon, cuz?"

Fenn's hackles rose. "I'm taking Neita to meet the Dobermans," he said coolly—and on the spur of the moment. Actually he *had* intended to return to his room. Or did he mean *retreat?*

Retreat from whom? he asked himself. From Weslin? Emily? Certainly not. And retreating from Neita might prove impossible since it seemed she was going to be his shadow.

What the hell's wrong with you, Volan? he demanded. Why are you letting a touch of amnesia turn you into a coward?

"Ready, Neita?" he asked.

She nodded, following him to the back door without comment.

"See you later," Weslin said in farewell.

Not knowing what his reaction might be, Fenn took a deep breath as he stepped over the threshold and found himself in the open. The day was cool and partly cloudy, but just as he emerged from under the protective overhang sheltering the back door, the sun, as though welcoming him, slid from behind a cloud to brighten the morning.

When he realized he wasn't going to panic, his heart lifted and he felt as elated as a boy leaving school for the summer vacation. He grinned at Neita, saying, "What a glorious day!"

Her smile lit her face, bringing a sparkle to her somber gray eyes. "Arranged especially for you, believe it or not."

Pleased with himself and delighted with her, he had a sudden impulse to pull her into his arms and taste the sweet mystery of her lips.

Definitely not a good idea, Volan, he reminded himself. Not yet, anyway. But it made him wish he hadn't been so quick to invite his cousins to the picnic.

The Dobermans were in their large pen at the rear of the house, the gate to the pen shackled by a chain and padlock. "Zorn is the male, the bigger of the two," Fenn commented as they neared the wire fencing. "His name means *anger* in German, and he lives up to it if he hasn't been properly introduced to you. They were trained as guard dogs."

Both of the identically marked brown-and-black dogs stared through the fencing at them, watching and waiting, not growling but not overly friendly, either. "The smaller dog is Zier, the female," Fenn said.

"Does her name have a meaning?" Neita asked.

"Ornament," Fenn said, smiling, "but no one's told her."

When they reached the fence, Fenn held out his hand for the dogs to sniff and then grasped Neita's hand, bringing it near the fence while clasped in his. "Friend," he said. "Friend."

Both dogs smelled her hand. When they were finished, Neita pulled free of him and crouched until her head was on the level of the dogs' heads. *"Komea,"* she intoned, and began whispering to them in a language he didn't understand. Zier capitulated first, wagging her stub of a tail and trying to lick Neita's face through the wire fencing.

Zorn took longer to come around but eventually he, too, began to show Neita that he'd not only accepted her but actually liked her.

"What did you do to them?" Fenn asked, amazed. "I've never seen them that friendly."

She bid the dogs goodbye and rose. "I told them they were superb animals and that I admired them very much and then—" She paused. "Don't laugh, but when I was a little girl, my Grandmother Metsula taught me a charm to use when I was confronted by strange animals. I just sort of automatically still do it."

"All this was in Finn, I take it."

"I've never tried to translate the charm into English." She slanted him a half smile. "Maybe I wouldn't be able to believe it would work if the words were in English, and if I couldn't believe in the charm, then it definitely wouldn't work."

He eyed her curiously. "Do you believe the charm works in Finnish?"

She shrugged. "The Dobermans seemed to think so."

Whether they always worked or not, Neita had been taught words to charm a savage beast, he mused. She also slept with a silver dagger under her pillow. Could it be possible Uncle Theo suspected what was troubling him? He doubted it, even though his uncle had claimed he was looking for "someone special" to replace Jethro. Still, Theo *had* found Neita, and the longer Fenn knew her, the more unusual he found her.

Unusual or not, how long would she be safe at Halfmoon House? What good were Finnish charms against what he feared might happen each time the moon was full?

On the way back to the house, he asked, "Are you from around here?"

"I moved to Eureka from the Bay Area about a month ago."

"Any particular reason?"

Neita hesitated before replying since she wasn't about to tell him she was running away from her own past. In any case, she wasn't exactly certain why she'd chosen to go north rather than south or east.

"Maybe it was the fog," she said. "Someone once told me Eureka was the fog capital of the world."

"I'm not sure that makes sense."

"It probably doesn't. But my Finnish namesake is Terhen Neiti, the Fog Maiden, and I suppose that might have influenced me. The subconscious is strange territory."

"Tell me." His voice was bleak. "Your Fog Maiden seems to have taken up permanent residence in mine."

She shook her head. "Temporary, I feel sure. You must know how closely the body and the mind are interlinked, but do you realize you've hardly been limping since we came outside?"

He shot her an amazed glance. After a moment he said, "You're right about the limp, and I can't deny you were right about forcing me to leave my room. But here's a question you can't answer. How do you or I know that I wouldn't be better off if I never recovered the memories I've lost?"

CHAPTER FOUR

The gazebo, instead of being gingerbread Victorian like the house, had columns and classic lines, reminding Neita of a small Roman temple. Situated on a knoll, it commanded a breathtaking view in all directions. As she turned to the west she saw, past a sweep of lawn and below rocky cliffs, the blue-green waters of the Pacific with a gray fog bank hovering far offshore.

Fenn, standing next to her, said, "Apparently my ancestors tended toward caution—no perching on the edge of a cliff with the waves pounding beneath for them. They built well back from the ocean. If the wind's right, sometimes you can hear the waves."

"I didn't realize Halfmoon House was the family homestead," she said.

"My great-grandfather built it, my grandfather inherited it, and my father and his two brothers grew up here. Only Uncle Theo stayed on."

Glancing around, Neita noticed Lycia and Weslin coming toward the gazebo and told Fenn. He continued to stare off to the west, giving no sign he'd heard her.

"The cliff," he muttered.

She waited, but when he didn't go on, she asked, "What about the cliff?"

He turned to look at her and shook his head. "I thought for a moment I was remembering something. Whatever it was, it's gone now. Maybe if I went to the sea cliffs..."

"You forgot wine," Weslin called, brandishing a bottle.

"And glasses," Lycia added as the twins climbed the steps of the gazebo. "We've brought both. After all, this *is* a celebration."

Weslin uncorked the wine, a Pinot blanc from a local vineyard, and poured it into the stemmed glasses Lycia had set on the glass-topped wicker table.

"Remember," Lycia said as she handed a glass to Fenn, "when we were teenagers we used to sneak out here at night with a bottle of wine? Why is the forbidden so much more fun?"

"Teenagers tend to rebel against rules," Neita said as she accepted a glass from Weslin. Though she had no intention of drinking the wine while she was acting as Fenn's nurse, she didn't want to make an issue of it.

Lycia raised her eyebrows. "You mistook my meaning. I'm well past adolescence, thank God, but I still do prefer the forbidden. It has such a delightfully dangerous ambience. Don't you think so, Fenn?"

He shrugged and took a sip of wine. "This is my first drink since the accident."

"Any luck remembering what happened?" Weslin asked.

"No, not really."

"Surely you'll get your memory back someday, won't you?" Lycia asked.

"The doctor refused to predict either if or when." Fenn's tone was dismissive.

Lycia wasn't easily discouraged. "What do you think, Neita?" she asked.

"Amnesia can be tricky," Neita said briefly.

"Could be your doctor's merely trying to cover his butt," Weslin put in. "My firm is loaded with malpractice suits."

"But Fenn doesn't really have amnesia, does he?" Lycia persisted, her yellow gaze shifting to Neita. "I mean, he knows who he is and who we are and all."

Feeling she had to respond, Neita tried to make her explanation as succinct as possible. "The time period amnesia can cover may be years or merely hours. People can forget everything, many things or only one specific thing."

"And sometimes the memory or memories are gone for good?" Lycia asked.

"That can happen," Neita said reluctantly, wishing they'd take the hint Fenn had given them and end the discussion. "But it usually doesn't."

Weslin clapped Fenn on the shoulder. "So don't worry, cuz. Sooner or later you—"

Fenn's scowl stopped him in midstream.

Lycia set her empty glass on the table and flung her arms around Fenn. "Poor baby, are we picking on you?"

He extricated himself, walked to the table and poured more wine into his glass, refilling Weslin's and Lycia's, too. Neita politely refused.

Weslin raised his glass, "To the Volans," he said. "May we all live long and prosper."

"We're the end of the Volan line," Lycia said after draining her glass and setting it down. "The last three." She put one arm around her brother's waist and the other around Fenn's. "Volans stand together!"

"Through thick and thin, through fire and flood," Weslin intoned.

"Through good and bad, we share the blood," Fenn chanted.

Watching them, Neita realized she must be listening to an adolescent ritual. It made her realize how close they must be and how much of an outsider she was. What a handsome trio they were, Lycia and Weslin smiling, Fenn somber, two brunettes and a blonde, all strikingly good-looking.

At thirty, though, they *weren't* the end of the Volan line. Surely there'd be children....

Neita turned away. She took a deep breath and let it out slowly, blinking back threatening tears as she wondered how long it was going to take her to get over what had happened to her the day Patrick died.

"High school was a lot of laughs," Lycia was saying to Fenn when Neita looked at them again. "I remember cheering at football games when you broke through the line and raced down the field with the opposing pack chasing you and the crowd chanting, 'Go, Fenris! Go, Fenris!'"

"Don't call me that!" Fenn snapped, pulling away from her. "It's not my name."

"Hey, take it easy, cuz," Weslin said. "She's only reminiscing."

Rather than chiding Fenn, Neita thought, Weslin ought to keep in mind that Fenn was still convalescent and remind his sister not to say things that might be upsetting. At the same time, she realized there could be undertones here she was missing because she was an outsider.

Lycia sauntered over to the table, poured the remaining wine into her glass and raised it. "To the Volan motto, to *Cave lupum,*" she said, her yellow eyes glowing as she stared at Fenn.

"That's enough!" Weslin cried, striding to his sister and jerking the glass from her hand. Gripping her arm, he propelled her down the stairs and onto the lawn, pulling her with him toward the house. Her laughter drifted back to the gazebo.

Fenn, unmoving, stared after the twins, his face darkened by such a ferocious scowl that Neita prudently remained silent.

In her nurse's training, she'd learned enough medical Latin to understand Lycia's challenging toast had been in that ancient language, but she didn't know the meaning of the words—though they sounded familiar.

Lupum sounded like *lupus,* a collagen disease. The words were so close they had to be related. If only she could remember why the disease was called lupus....

Fenn whirled, stalked to the railing and gazed unseeingly at the distant ocean, vaguely aware that the offshore fog bank was creeping toward the land. Why the hell had he reacted so strongly to what Lycia had called him? It had only provoked her to go further. He should have laughed it off. Laughing at Lycia had always been the best way to deal with her.

Too bad there was so little laughter left in him.

For a few moments it had almost been like old times when the three of them were close, but then that crazy childhood rhyme of theirs had echoed and reechoed in his head, the words no longer a bond, no longer amusing but somehow sinister. And then Lycia had attacked him in her own special, underhanded, "just teasing" way.

He knew why. She was annoyed with him because when she'd crawled into his bed this morning he'd refused to play games. Flight was the easiest way out so he'd retired to the bathroom and locked himself in.

At sixteen he hadn't found it so simple. One night in this same damn gazebo, he'd come close to succumbing. A nagging sense of wrongness, the feeling that he was making love to a girl he regarded as his sister had finally overcome his teenage lust. He'd felt guilty until Lycia had tried to seduce him at a friend's party. Then he belatedly realized what had happened in the gazebo had been at least as much her fault as his.

After the second time he refused, she'd never come on to him quite so blatantly again and, eventually, they'd gone their separate ways. Now, when they met, she made a point of warm cousinly affection, but he remained wary. Lycia was not the forgiving type. If she didn't get what she wanted, she always found a way to get even.

Did she suspect what was troubling him? He didn't see how she could have any idea, even though Lycia was an expert at ferreting out the secrets of others.

Fenn slammed his fist against one of the gazebo pillars. "I've *got* to remember," he muttered.

"I've laid out the food if you care to eat," Neita said from behind him.

He'd all but forgotten she was there. He turned, frowning, ready to say to hell with the food. She stood by the table, her expression revealing nothing, her gray eyes unreadable. It crossed his mind that she somehow looked untouched, as though she'd never been buffeted by the ill winds of the world.

"Shall we plan a walk to the sea cliffs tomorrow?" she asked.

If she'd urged him to eat, he would have refused. Instead, he found himself saying, "Your eyes give nothing away. It makes me wonder what you're feeling."

She smiled slightly. "At the moment I'm trying to decide if it's possible to keep myself from grabbing one of Emily's baked-ham-on-rye sandwiches while I wait for you to make up your mind whether to snarl at me or to start eating."

One side of his mouth curled up. "And?"

"Politeness loses, hunger wins." As she spoke she reached for a sandwich.

Amused, he took one, too, and bit into it, savoring the tang of Emily's special mustard. Nodding toward a wicker chair, he said, "Since I've given up on snarling, we may as well be comfortable."

As they continued to eat, he began to realize just how comfortable he was, and he knew it was because Neita was with him. Though there'd been no recurrence of that strange and disconcertingly intense flash of desire he'd experienced the first time he touched her, he couldn't help wondering what would happen if he kissed her.

The white shirt she wore revealed no secrets, but when she'd come into his room last night in her robe, even in his distraction he'd noted the enticing fullness of her breasts. And her lower lip had a sensuous curve that suggested passion could warm those cool gray eyes.

She reached for an almond cookie and he gazed at her hand—small but square and capable-looking with short, neatly trimmed nails that were unpolished, the way he liked them. Belatedly remembering what he'd seen on that hand when they met, he grasped it involuntarily and stared at her palm, unsure what to expect but needing to know.

"What do you see?" she asked.

"Nothing but skin." Did the relief he felt show in his voice?

"Do you read palms?"

He dropped her hand. "No, I don't." Turning away, he noticed the fog had reached the sea cliffs. "We should pack up and go back to the house," he said, "before we become fogbound."

"Does it really get that thick?" she asked as she rose and began clearing away the food.

"Sometimes." He brought the picnic basket to the table and, as he watched her deftly repack it, he suddenly realized where his intense dislike of painted fingernails must have come from. It could only be a result of that day in the attic when he was a boy and Aunt Hensa had traced a star within a circle on his friend Donny's hand with one long red fingernail, a fingernail as red as blood.

He abruptly left the table and stalked to the rail, his back to Neita. Only Aunt Hensa had been able to see that pentagram—but that hadn't saved Donny. And last night Fenn had been the only one to see the pentagram on Neita's palm....

"Hallucination," he muttered. "I didn't really see anything."

"What didn't you see?" Neita spoke from beside him.

"You move like a cat," he said harshly, annoyed because she'd both startled him and overheard him talking to himself. "Too damn quietly. I didn't hear you."

"I guess you were too preoccupied to notice. I wasn't trying to be quiet. Everything's packed and ready."

Neita recognized fear when she saw it. Something had spooked Fenn, driving him away from the table. Thinking back, she decided it couldn't have been anything she'd said. What was left? Did the fog pose some sort of threat to him? Or was it that business with the palm of her hand, echoing his behavior of the night before?

Hallucination.

What had he seen or thought he'd seen? And how could it be connected with the palm of her hand? Or the fog? Instead of sharing his fear with her, he covered it up with gruffness. Unless he was willing to open up and trust her, she couldn't help him.

As they descended the gazebo steps, tentacles of fog coiled around them. Already the sun was hidden, bringing a coolness to the afternoon. Neita made up her mind to be blunt.

"Does the fog bother you?" she asked.

He glanced at her, eyebrows raised. "Fog bother a Eurekan? Don't forget I grew up here. You Bay Area people may think you have a corner on fog, but compared to us, you guys don't have a clue what fog is really like. We've got the thickest and the longest lasting."

By the time they reached the house, she was totally convinced that, rather than being afraid of it, he was actually proud of Eureka's fog. Neita crossed it off her list. If only she could talk to Fenn's doctor, she might have more of an idea what was troubling her patient. But Fenn had been hospitalized at Stanford so the physicians who really knew his case were in Palo Alto, not Eureka, and she didn't know their names. She could, of course, try tackling Fenn's Uncle Theo. Or the twins.

She frowned, aware she'd be reluctant to go behind Fenn's back to ask questions of his cousins. And she knew she'd have reservations about whatever they told her. For some illogical reason, she felt she was ranged on Fenn's side, the two of them standing against Lycia and Weslin.

Uncle Theo, though, was on Fenn's side, too. He must be or he wouldn't have hired her.

Chances were she was wrong about the twins. They'd grown up with Fenn, and the three of them obviously shared many fond memories of their youth together. What was that childish jingle of theirs?

Through thick and thin, through fire and flood
Through good and bad, we share the blood....

Neita sighed. It must be great to have siblings or close cousins. Only children, like herself, might get more adult attention, but she'd still been lonely as a little girl.

They reached the back door and Fenn shifted his cane to open it. With his hand on the knob, he paused. "Tonight," he said, "my friend, the fog will hide the moon. You and I should both sleep well."

He was wrong.

The night started off well enough. Fenn retired before ten, so Neita had no qualms about crawling into her own bed soon afterward. As she lay on her back, yearning for sleep's elusive embrace and puzzling over Fenn's comment about the fog being his friend, she noticed a thin vapor drifting across the room from her window. Though she'd opened it only a crack, apparently that was enough to let the fog in. She frowned, unable to recall fog ever coming inside before.

The gray wisps seemed to gather into a shapeless, elongated figure that floated above the foot of her bed. At the same time, words formed in her mind. *Child who is my namesake, beware. The wolves gather.*

Neita blinked, then sat up, hugging herself and shivering as she stared toward the foot of her bed. Nothing remained of the misty figure. Had she actually seen something or had she begun to doze and had a hallucinatory half dream?

Grandma Metsula might have believed Terhen Neiti existed, Neita told herself, but the Fog Maiden really was nothing but a Finnish myth. A myth—not reality. She'd dreamed. That's all there was to it.

But the warning replayed over and over in her mind. *The wolves gather.* What did it mean? In spite of the howling she'd heard on the previous night, she knew California had no wolves. It was possible, though, that the howling had pried the warning from some deep layer of her subconscious. Or even her unconscious, where racial memories hid. Her Finnish ancestors, living in snowbound forest homes, must have feared the winter wolves.

That thought triggered her memory. The disease called lupus was so named because patients who suffered from it often had facial lesions that gave them a wolflike appearance. *Lupus* meant *wolf*. By extension, the *lupum* from the toast Lycia had proposed—*Cave lupum*—would also mean *wolf*.

Which meant—what? In all likelihood, nothing. There was little to be gained by making false assumptions. Even so, her thoughts circled around and around the wolf theme like, she told herself wryly, a wolf cub chasing its tail. When she finally settled down once again, it took her some time to slip into an uneasy sleep.

Dreaming, Neita thought someone was calling her name. No, not her name. Another's. Calling and calling. She woke with a start and was immediately certain someone was in her room.

"Donny," a voice said. "Come back, Donny."

She lay tense and unmoving for a moment, blinking in confusion. Whoever spoke sounded like a boy, but there were no boys at Halfmoon House. Cautiously she raised her head, peering fearfully into the darkness.

She felt rather than saw something slip past her bed in the direction of her windows. Fenn? When she heard the creak of a window being raised, she sat up and quickly slid from the bed. Those long windows led to the little balcony off her bedroom. Fearing now for

Fenn rather than herself, she flicked on her bedside lamp and hurried to the window. Fenn, wearing only pajama bottoms, had already stepped over the sill onto the balcony.

"Fenn," she said urgently. When he didn't respond, she knew he was sleepwalking again.

She followed him onto the balcony, standing beside him in the foggy night without touching him. He turned toward her, his eyes pits of darkness in the dim light filtering through the curtains.

"You killed him," he said in a child's voice.

For one wild, irrational moment, she believed he was accusing her of killing Patrick, and she froze. Wrong or right, she blamed herself for Patrick's death.

"I hate you, Aunt Hensa," Fenn went on in his child's voice.

His words jolted through her, freeing her from the guilt of her own past while alerting her to possible danger from Fenn's past. In his somnambulistic state, he must believe himself to be a child again and her to be his hated aunt. But he wasn't a child—he was a man, with a man's strength.

Nothing she might say would break through his trance. He was following his own childhood scenario, not really seeing or hearing her.

"I saw you." His voice dropped to a whisper. "I saw what you did to Donny." Quick as a striking snake, his hand whipped out and grasped hers, turning it palm upward.

With his forefinger, he traced a symbol onto her palm—a star, she thought, surrounded by a circle. Though the invisible drawing had no meaning for her, a sense of evil raised the hair on her nape. She tried to free her hand. His grip tightened.

"That time you let him go," Fenn whispered. "But I watched you 'cause I knew you were like a cat playing with its prey. I saw you come back that night with Donny's blood smeared on your face. He was my best friend and you killed him." As he forced Neita against the iron rail of the balcony, his voice, still that of a boy, rose. "I wish you were dead, dead, dead!"

With his weight pinning her against the metal, her frantic struggle was of no avail. What would he do next? Tip her up and over the rail? Even if she survived the fall from the second story, she was sure to be seriously injured. She tried to think what to do, but the similarity of her frightful predicament to those final nightmare moments with Patrick threw her mind into panic.

She was doomed.

CHAPTER FIVE

Shoved up against the cold iron of the balcony railing by Fenn, Neita despaired. Since he was so much stronger than she, her only chance was to shock him from his somnambulistic state. But how?

"Fenn!" she cried.

As she feared, he didn't react to his name, but from the foggy depths below she heard a muffled growl. The dogs! She'd forgotten they patrolled the grounds at night.

"Zorn!" she called in desperation. "Zier! Help me!"

From below, paws scratched against the side of the house as the dogs tried futilely to reach the balcony. A fury of barking and snarling broke out.

Fenn's grip relaxed abruptly, freeing Neita's wrists. She pushed her hands against his chest, shoving him away from her, then retreated to the window leading into her room.

"What—what happened?" he asked, his voice once again his own—a man's voice, not a boy's. "Why are we on the balcony? And what's wrong with the dogs?" He leaned over the rail and called to them.

The barking stopped.

Certain now that he was awake and aware once again, Neita said, "We'd better go inside." She climbed over the low sill, crossed to her bed and slumped onto it, still weak in the knees from her fright.

Fenn followed, closing the window behind him. By the time she'd pulled her robe around herself, he was standing over her.

"I must have walked in my sleep again," he said. "Right?"

"Who is Donny?" she blurted, her nerves too raw to make her careful about what she asked him. "And who is Aunt Hensa?"

He stared at her without answering.

"Damn it," she snapped, "tell me! You scared me half to death out there on the balcony."

A muscle twitched in his jaw. "I didn't know what I was doing and I still don't know what I did. But I'm sorry."

"You're still making me nervous looming over me like that," she said crossly. He turned away without replying, obviously intending to return to his own room. She caught his hand, stopping him. "Oh, no, you don't. You're not getting away without answering my question." She tugged at his hand until he eased down next to her on the bed. "Tell me," she demanded.

He sighed. "I can't."

"You must. How can I help you if you won't let me know what's troubling you?"

"No one can help me." He gazed at her, his green eyes cloudy. "I told you when we met to leave Half-moon House. You refused. Now that you've learned it's dangerous for you to be around me, I hope you've changed your mind."

Neita looked into his eyes, trying to see beyond the greenness, trying to sense shadow. She could not. Even on the balcony, when he was so threatening, she hadn't felt any darkness within him. Though there *had* been evil present.

She reached for his hand, turned it palm upward and, with her forefinger, traced the strange symbol on his palm, saying, "This is what you did to me on the balcony."

He jerked his hand free. "How much do you know about pentagrams?" he asked harshly.

"I never heard the word before, but I do know one thing. When you, believing I was Aunt Hensa, drew the pentagram on my palm, I felt a chill, a wrongness. Just now, drawing it on yours, I felt nothing."

"Go home, Neita." His voice was hoarse. "Go, before it's too late."

There was no denying she was tempted to leave. Though she had no fear of Fenn at this moment, she'd been terrified on the balcony. What should she do? Why did she feel so positive she and she alone could save him? This instinctive sense of hers was as intense as it was inexplicable. Even though she didn't yet understand what he must be saved from, she knew if she deserted him now she'd never forgive herself.

"It's already too late," she said, laying her hand on his arm.

She thought she meant only to soothe him with her touch, but when he grasped her hand and brought it to his lips, the thrill that quivered through her told her she was wrong. She'd touched him because she needed to touch him, and also because she wanted him to touch her.

The warmth of his lips on her palm seared along her nerves, triggering the heat of desire. No, she thought in dismay. No. I can't get involved in this way. Not with Fenn.

"Neita?" he asked in a husky whisper.

The longing in his voice undid her, scattering her reason, evoking her own need. When he reached for her, she melted into his arms. His mouth covered hers, trapping her in a spiraling surge of desire she found impossible to resist.

From the instant they first touched and invisible flames sizzled between them, she'd known in her heart of hearts that neither of them had a choice. Nothing remotely like it had ever happened to her before. She'd always been in control, always had a choice. No longer.

Never mind that he was a dark, enigmatic, sometimes dangerous stranger. She'd chosen him. Or, more accurately, he'd been chosen *for* her, whether she wished it or not.

"Fate is capricious," Grandma Metsula had told her long ago. "Even the most skilled *noita* can't alter fate."

Though she seemed to have some small skills, Neita knew she was far from being a true *noita,* the Finnish name for a witch or wizard. If fate intended her to be in Fenn's arms, she had to admit she was more than willing.

Fenn stretched out on the bed, bringing Neita with him, molding her body to his. I shouldn't be doing this, he told himself.

But he knew he had no intention of stopping. He needed her desperately; he'd never wanted a woman more. She was fire, the flame of life itself. He'd been inescapably drawn to her from the first; they shared a strange bonding he didn't understand.

The mystifying past, the terrifying present and the sinister future vanished. Nothing mattered but holding her, kissing her, relishing the sweet softness of her breasts under his hands and her muted gasps of pleasure. Nothing existed except their lovemaking.

If he could, he'd make it last forever. He'd keep them both in the fantasy world of passion and desire, where there was no tomorrow.

He breathed in her arousing scent—more spicy than sweet, but at the same time indefinable—a scent as elusive as the fog. She tasted like the honey distilled from some unknown exotic flower that grew in a wild and secret glen, and no other woman's skin had ever felt so petal-smooth. He'd never have enough of touching her.

Her lips, warm and ardent against his, opened invitingly, making his heart pound. Eagerly he explored the tempting secrets of her mouth, her soft moans driving him up and up, fragmenting his control, infusing him with an insistent need to possess her.

He'd been a long time without a woman, but that wasn't the reason he couldn't wait. She wasn't merely a woman to him, she was *the* woman and her evident desire for him drove him closer and closer to the edge. He wanted all of her, and he wanted it now. Nothing would stop him.

But as they clung together, their clothes discarded, she murmured his name and he heard the plea in her passion-blurred voice. A plea for him to stop? He brushed the possibility aside. She wanted what he wanted; she could only be asking him to take them both on a lover's journey to a place they'd never been, a place they would never find without each other.

He was rising above her when he felt her tense. She drew in her breath so sharply the sound penetrated his daze of desire, making him aware something was wrong. Only then did he notice the moonlight slanting across the bed, and he realized the fog had lifted. Only then did he hear the sound he dreaded. He froze, all desire vanishing.

Somewhere in the night a creature sang to the moon. Sang to him. The eldritch howling came from the throat of no dog or coyote or wolf. Though he didn't know what it was that howled in the moonlit darkness, he knew it was no known animal that called to him.

He shifted position and sat up, listening against his will to the urgent summons, feeling the eerie notes taint and sicken him like a subtle poison. He started to rise from the bed.

"No!" From behind him, Neita wrapped her arms around his chest, preventing him from getting to his feet, determined not to let him out of her sight. Without any proof, she was convinced Fenn might venture into the night to go to the source of the howling.

"If you know what it is that howls, for God's sake, tell me," she pleaded.

When Fenn didn't struggle to free himself, she released her grip, keeping one hand on his arm. Still naked, he sat stiffly and silently on the edge of her bed—listening, she was sure. She listened, too. The next time the howling came, the sound was fainter, farther away.

She shook his arm. "Speak to me!" she demanded.

"I don't know what it is." His voice was flat.

"And yet you were thinking about leaving the house, weren't you?"

As if her question broke his trance, he retrieved his pajama bottoms from the floor and slid them on. Neita released him and yanked her nightgown back on. She refused to allow herself to think about what had happened between them or what the howling had prevented from happening—now wasn't the time.

"Yes," he admitted, "I was thinking about it. I have before. But I've stayed inside. So far." He slanted her a look. "It's calling me, you know."

"Why?"

He shrugged.

"Do you connect the howling in some way with your lost memory?"

He swiveled to face her. "Damn it, how do I know?" His voice bristled with anger.

"So you're afraid there's a connection," she said calmly. "Does this have anything to do with Donny and the pentagram and Aunt Hensa? I won't accept silence. I'm not leaving Halfmoon House, but that doesn't mean I won't try to protect myself. After the fright you gave me on the balcony, surely you understand why you must share at least some of this with me."

"I don't know what happened on the balcony," he said, "but you do deserve an answer. Keep in mind that I was only five when Donny disappeared, so what I tell you is a child's view of what might have occurred. Donny was my friend, we were the same age.

Aunt Hensa was Lycia and Weslin's mother and she was staying with my parents for some reason. At five, I didn't know why. Now I suspect she and my uncle Leon had a falling-out over her—peculiarities. In any case, my cousins weren't at our house with her but at home with their father.''

His gaze shifted from her and he stared at the moonlit swath crossing the bed. "Uncle Leon was all right, but I didn't like Aunt Hensa—I was afraid of her. When she came to the attic where Donny and I were playing, she scared me. Donny seemed to like her, though, even after she traced a pentagram on his palm, claiming she saw it there."

He paused for so long she began to wonder if he meant to continue. "So that was why you drew the pentagram on my hand while we were on the balcony," she said finally. "You were calling me Aunt Hensa at the time."

A brief spasm of pain tightened his face. He took a deep breath and shook his head. "I've never told anyone about Aunt Hensa coming to the attic and what she did then and what I believe she did later. Even thinking about it makes me feel like that frightened five-year-old all over again."

"Maybe if you did talk about it, you wouldn't have to reenact the past while you sleepwalk," she said.

His nod was slow and reluctant. "You may be right. I've already put you at risk—I have no choice but to tell you."

He rose and began pacing while she propped herself up on pillows and waited. He completed two turns before pausing beside the bed, gazing beyond her as if looking into the past.

"After she traced the pentagram," he said hesitantly, "Aunt Hensa smiled at Donny while she told him that he couldn't escape. Then she hugged and kissed him and went away." Fenn resumed pacing before continuing. "Donny left before dark, and she must have waited for him somewhere between my house and his, because he didn't go home. His parents called mine to find out where Donny was, and soon after the police arrived and asked questions.

"Aunt Hensa wasn't there when the police came. In the way little kids sometimes know things—without any proof—I knew she'd caught Donny and that I'd never see him again. I've always felt guilty because I didn't speak up. But who'd believe a five-year-old? Besides, I was afraid of what Aunt Hensa might do to me. So I said nothing.

"I couldn't sleep, though I pretended to when my mother came in and kissed me good-night before she went to bed. My father didn't come in to kiss me so I knew he was still up. Hoping he wouldn't notice me, I crept from my room and sat on the top step of the staircase, scared but determined to wait there until Aunt Hensa came home. The lights were all off downstairs, and I remember the full moon shining in through the landing window and the entry windows below, turning the steps to silver."

Fenn paused by the windows as though reluctant to walk across the swath of moonlight on the floor. "My father must have heard her coming before I did," he said as he resumed pacing, "because suddenly he strode from the living room into the entry and stood by the door. I scrunched up small against the newel post, but he didn't so much as glance at the staircase.

Aunt Hensa's key clicked in the lock and the door swung open. When I saw that she wore what I thought of as a dark witch's cape, I was terrified and I put my hand over my mouth to prevent my squeak of fright from being heard.

"'You've lied to me,' my father told her, his voice so cold and hard I shivered. 'I should have known what was wrong when you ran out on Leon.'

"Aunt Hensa laughed. 'Leon's a fool,' she said.

"Father shook his head. 'He's no fool, except where you're concerned. I warned Leon it was risky to marry a woman who carried Volan genes, but he was besotted with you.'

"She laughed again, triumphant, head thrown back, her eyes glittering in the moonlight. 'You wanted me yourself. You still do.' She flung off the black cloak and I muffled a gasp with my hand. Aunt Hensa was naked.

"She raised her arms in invitation to my father, and for a long and dreadful moment I feared he was going to hug her like he did my mother. Looking back, I realize he must have been tempted. I feared and hated her, but even at five I knew she was beautiful in some strange way that other women weren't.

"My father stepped back, his face twisted with distaste. 'I'd sooner embrace a snake,' he'd said, his voice quivering. 'Get the hell out of my sight; I never want to see you again. I give you five minutes to pack and leave my house. And good God, woman, wash the blood off your face before you go.'

"Then I understood that the dark smears around her mouth were Donny's blood and I knew he was dead. I fled, diving into my mother's bed. Even snuggled up against my mother, I didn't feel safe. Aunt Hensa might be gone from our house, but as long as she was alive there was nowhere I was safe.''

Fenn stopped by the bed again, a muscle twitching in his cheek. Neita stared at him, speechless with horrified pity for the boy he'd been.

''Two weeks later,'' he said, ''my uncle Leon asked my father to his house and my mother insisted on going along. Since Donny's death I'd become an eavesdropper, and so I'd learned that Aunt Hensa had gone back to Leon. After my father had told him what she'd done, Uncle Leon locked Aunt Hensa in her room. The conference was to decide what to do with her. Before my parents left, Uncle Theo—who knew nothing about all this—arrived in San Mateo, saying, as he had for the past two summers, that he'd come to collect his nephews and his niece and take them for a week's visit at his place.

''While the three of us were with Uncle Theo in Eureka, Uncle Leon's house burned, killing my parents as well as Lycia's and Weslin's. I've always believed Aunt Hensa set that fire.''

Neita quelled her impulse to jump up and put her arms around him. It was risky to touch Fenn that intimately—what was meant as comfort might all too easily mutate into another emotion entirely.

''What a dreadful secret for a little boy to have to cope with,'' she said. ''And then to lose your parents, besides.'' Despite her overwhelming sympathy, though, she couldn't rid herself of an uneasy feeling he'd left something out. Granted it was terrible that his aunt had killed his friend, but why did she have blood on her mouth afterward? And what did the penta-gram have to do with the killing?

She reached for his hand and gripped it, intending a brief, comforting contact. His fingers closed around hers, and then he pulled her from the bed onto her feet.

"You've complained about me looming over you," he said with a half smile, "and this seemed less dangerous than the alternative."

His eyes, she thought bemusedly as she stared into them, were the green of new spring leaves. She knew she ought to step back and away from him instead of standing so close she could almost feel the warmth of his body, but she didn't move. No man had ever affected her the way Fenn did. When she gazed into his eyes, she forgot her misgivings, forgot why she was here, forgot everything but the need to be in his arms....

"If you keep looking at me like that," he said, letting his hands come to rest on her shoulders, "my good intentions will take flight."

Touching her again was a mistake, Fenn told himself, but he did nothing to correct the error. Instead he slid his hands down her back, drawing her closer. Her eyes, gray as fog, held the promise of forgetfulness. He could lose himself forever in those eyes.

No matter how many times he warned himself about the risk of keeping her near him, the truth was he couldn't bear to see her go. She offered more than the heady thrill of lovemaking; in her arms he sensed he could find that elusive something he'd been searching for all his life.

With his hands molding the arousing curve of her hips, how could he worry about hallucinations? A pentagram was a symbol without meaning compared to the fullness of her breasts pressing sensuously against his bare chest. He wanted her with an intensity beyond anything he'd ever experienced.

He brushed his lips over hers, the tip of his tongue savoring her taste.

She sighed, a whisper of sound against his lips. "I vowed never to get involved with a patient," she said.

"I'd rather be your lover," he told her, and captured her mouth with his.

Entranced by the pleasure of caressing her, as well as his escalating desire, he didn't connect the distant pounding with someone knocking. Not until Neita broke free of his embrace.

"Someone's at your door," she said.

Muttering, he padded through to his room and flung the door open. What the hell happened now? Barnes, his gray hair awry and looking more agitated than Fenn had ever seen him, said, "Sorry to disturb you, but I didn't want to rouse your uncle—he wasn't feeling well earlier. I've just come from outside. Something attacked the dogs. Zier isn't badly hurt, but Zorn—" Barnes's voice quavered. "He's pretty well been torn to pieces."

"Oh, no!" Neita cried from behind him. "The beast got poor Zorn." Barnes glanced at her, then quickly away.

"The dogs were barking earlier," Fenn said, "but I didn't hear anything that sounded like a fight."

"Nor did I," Barnes agreed. "Zier woke me by whining and scratching on the back door—my bedroom's close by, as you know. When I went to see what was wrong, I saw she was covered with blood. I called Zorn, but when he didn't come, I let Zier into the kitchen and took care of her injury—a small gash on one shoulder. I realized then all that blood couldn't have come from her. As soon as I finished, she went straight to the door and whined to be let out." He broke off, his gaze sliding away from Fenn's. "I knew she'd lead me to Zorn, but I admit I waited some time before I could bring myself to open that door and follow her."

Fenn laid his hand on Barnes's shoulder. "I don't blame you."

"When I did get up the nerve to go, I took along the gun Mr. Theo gave me some months ago."

Fenn blinked, unpleasantly surprised. How much did his uncle suspect? "What gun?" he demanded.

"It's a .38. I'm a fair shot with a revolver, as Mr. Theo can tell you. The gun was loaded when he handed it to me. 'Don't unload this,' he told me, 'and don't use any other ammunition.' I kept that gun in my hand while I followed Zier. Her injuries slowed her, and that, along with the full moon lighting my way, made her easy to keep in sight. She led me straight to Zorn—or what was left of him. I found his remains just inside the pine grove to the east of the grounds."

Fenn clenched his teeth, feeling chilled clear through to the bone.

"I'm telling you it was an awful sight," Barnes added, grimacing. "I could see that whatever it was that savaged poor Zorn must have eaten part of him."

"The beast," Neita whispered, hugging herself. "The thing that howls in the night."

Her gaze sought Fenn's, and the horror in her eyes made him look away, even though he knew it wasn't directed at him. What he feared was the possibility that one day it would be. And when that happened, there'd be no way to save her.

CHAPTER SIX

Neita woke to sunlight and a muted swish that she knew must be the shower in Fenn's bathroom. She rose, quickly bathed and pulled on a rose shirt and black twill pants. When she was dressed, she tapped on the connecting door, closed last night at Fenn's insistence.

"Coming to say goodbye?" he asked as he let her in. He wore dark green sweats and his eyes were cloudy and guarded.

"I'm here to remind you we're hiking to the sea cliffs this morning," she told him.

"I thought by now you'd be packed and ready to put Halfmoon House behind you."

"You don't listen, do you? I said I had no intention of leaving, and I keep my word." She refused to let him know how difficult a decision it had been for her to remain.

She knew there were things Fenn wasn't revealing, but what he had told her, plus what happened last night, was enough to convince her that he was in deadly peril. For some reason he believed the eerie howls were a summons he must answer. Her presence might be enough to prevent him. How could she take the chance that, if she left, he might venture into the night to look for the beast? She couldn't bear to think of him suffering Zorn's dreadful fate.

At the same time, she was determined not to allow herself to fall under the erotic spell he cast. After insisting that becoming involved with her patients wasn't on her agenda, she'd somehow managed to lose control of her emotions—not once but *twice* in the same night. That simply must not happen again. Would not.

Fenn shook his head. "You're the one who doesn't listen, Neita. You're not safe here."

She raised her chin. "Neither are you, so that makes two of us."

"I don't think you understand what I mean."

"Then explain."

He glared at her. "For God's sake, woman, *I'm* dangerous! Especially to you."

"Are you referring to your somnambulism?"

"That and more. Don't be so damn complacent. Medicine doesn't have all the answers, not by a long shot. You nurses can be insufferably smug."

Stung, she snapped, "I try to think rationally. Would you prefer to have me fearing you may turn into some kind of werewolf just because you're entertaining a delusion about that murderous beast calling you?"

The color drained from Fenn's face. Concern replaced Neita's annoyance. "Are you feeling faint?" she asked, taking his wrist to check his pulse. "Here, sit down."

He shook her off. "Nothing's wrong. Quit hovering and let me be alone for a few minutes. I'll join you downstairs for breakfast."

Since she had no excuse to refuse—his pulse had been strong and steady—Neita returned to her own room. Actually, she thought, it would be a good idea to go down before Fenn. She wanted to speak to his uncle Theo if at all possible.

"Sorry, Ms. Metsula," Barnes said when she found him downstairs. "Mr. Theo is still a bit under the weather. I'll let him know you want to see him, but I'd say it'll be no sooner than tomorrow before you'll have the chance."

"Is there anything I can do to make him more comfortable?" she asked, aware that Theo had recently recovered from a heart attack.

"I'm quite capable of caring for Mr. Theo." Barnes sounded a bit huffy.

"I'm sure you are," she said soothingly. "But if you ever do think he needs me, please don't hesitate to let me know."

"Of course."

When Emily discovered Fenn planned to eat with Neita, she insisted on serving them in what she called the morning room, located off the hall that led from the entry to the kitchen. Flowering plants hung from the ceiling, lending charm to the small, sunny room that was furnished with a glass-topped table and four chairs, plus an old-fashioned platform rocker by the oriel window where more plants grew.

"Seeing as how Ms. Lycia and Mr. Weslin left real early this morning, there'll only be the two of you in here," Emily said. "I've heard this was old Mrs. Volan's favorite room. I got to picturing her sitting in that rocker with maybe a cat purring on her lap, and I said so once to Mr. Theo." Emily shook her head. "Just goes to show you can't put any trust in imagination. Seems she was allergic to cats, just like Mr. Theo and the rest of the Volans. They can't abide a single cat in the house. Pity. I do miss the comfort of a cat somehow."

"Cats can be good company," Neita agreed. "Dogs, too." Reminded of what had happened to Zorn, and not wanting to distress Emily, she added, "Any pet, really."

She was too late. "I guess you and Mr. Fenn heard how poor Zorn got torn apart," Emily said. "Mr. Theo warned Barnes and me as how we wasn't to mention that critter out there howling when the moon's full, 'cause he didn't want Mr. Fenn upset. It's been going on for two months now, the howling. From the first, I didn't like listening to it nor having to keep it to myself. 'Bound to be trouble,' I told Barnes, and you see I was right—and Mr. Fenn smack in the midst. Mr. Theo won't like that, not at all."

"Does anyone know what kind of beast it is?"

Emily shook her head. "Not for sure. Some kind of wolf, I'd say. A while back, a certain person around here took to raising wolf pups from a female wolf they bred to an Alaskan husky, but the sheriff got after them and they had to get rid of the mother and the pups. Seems it's against the law to keep a wolf as a pet. Anyway, I bet one of them pups got loose and went wild."

Relief brought a smile to Neita's lips. While she couldn't be sure Emily's belief was correct, it was a reasonable explanation of where the night howler came from and what kind of an animal it was. Not that she'd thought there was anything unnatural about the howling, but the sound was enough to set anyone's nerves on edge. She could hardly wait to tell Fenn.

* * *

Using maximum self-control, Neita waited until she and Fenn had eaten their fill of Emily's loganberry waffles and were sitting back with second cups of coffee.

"A stray wolf dog?" he repeated incredulously when she finished telling him.

"Yes, that's Emily's story and there's no reason to doubt her."

"I suppose she could be right. God, how I hope she is. Because then *I'm* wrong."

"What did you think the animal was?" Neita asked curiously.

He shrugged. "It doesn't matter." He pushed his chair back from the table and rose. "Ask Emily for a couple of sandwiches and something to drink—nothing fancy or heavy to carry. I'll meet you in front of the house in fifteen minutes."

Later, as they walked side by side toward the cliffs overlooking the ocean, Neita remarked, "You're limping less."

He looked at her. "My leg's better. Maybe it's the exercise. Or the company. I didn't expect anyone like you. When Uncle Theo told me that my new nurse was on the way to Halfmoon House, I was damned annoyed. Even you'll have to admit I don't really need a nurse."

She raised her eyebrows but said nothing.

"I figured the nurse would be another Jethro," he went on. "Jethro was great when I needed help with what he called the 'activities of daily living'—God, how I hate jargon—but once I could do for myself, he wasn't much use. To tell the truth, I was relieved when he decided to disappear.''

Neita frowned. She'd never met Jethro, but his vanishing act bothered her. She recalled being told that Jethro had been hired through a medical registry, and it seemed odd that he'd risk his status with that agency by leaving a position without notice.

"Did he leave any of his belongings behind when he vanished?" she asked, curious to know how abrupt Jethro's departure might have been.

"If he did happen to, nobody ever told me." Fenn took a deep breath of the cool morning air. "I'd almost forgotten the smell of the sea. Makes me feel good to be alive."

"That's why I'm here," she said.

"To make me feel glad I'm alive?"

"Something like that, yes."

He caught her arm, halting her. "You've made me feel a hell of a lot more than glad." The husky note in his voice derailed her "never-again" resolve.

"If you're referring to what happened between us during the night," she said, putting herself firmly back on track, "that was a mistake I don't intend to make again."

He ran his forefinger down her cheek. "Good intentions lead you-know-where."

With his touch tingling through her, she fumbled for more dismissive words. "It *won't* happen again."

He grinned. "I've always enjoyed a challenge."

She hadn't yet come up with a response when his grin faded and his eyes grew blank, as though he were looking inward.

"Challenge," he repeated in a monotone. "I was challenged. To—to—" He blinked and then grimaced. "I almost had it, but now it's gone and I can't bring back the memory."

"Remembering can't be forced," she said. "Let's go on to the cliffs."

Ignoring her admonition, he muttered, "Challenge, challenge," as they began walking once more.

Neita knew from her medical training that his desperate attempt to retrieve what he'd lost of his past was not only counterproductive but might even prevent their walk on the cliffs from triggering a memory.

In an effort to distract him, she said, "I believe Lycia mentioned you were a jock in your high school days—did you go on to play football in college?"

"Football? No."

Wanting to keep his mind away from his amnesia, she sought something more to say. "I gather you must have been the star of your high school team. Didn't Lycia say the crowd cheered you, shouting your name when you carried the ball down the field?"

He turned and glared at her. "Fenris wasn't my name then and it isn't now!"

Taken aback, she said defensively, "*I* didn't call you Fenris."

Other than increasing his pace, he didn't respond. It wasn't until they reached the barren rock of the cliffs and paused near the edge to gaze out over the ocean that he spoke again.

"Sorry. For some reason I hated that name. Are you familiar with it?"

She shook her head.

"I thought you might be, because it comes from Norse mythology and you're Finnish."

"Finns aren't really Nordic," she said. "They're not related to Danes, Norwegians or Swedes. Finns are a unique people. Even their mythology is different from any other."

"In that case, I suppose I owe you an explanation. Fenris is the demon wolf who helps to bring about the downfall of the Norse gods and goddesses. He's an evil figure, a harbinger of doom."

Neita stole a sideways glance at Fenn and found him staring at the waves crashing against the rocks far below. Deciding silence was best, she said nothing, but kept watching him covertly. Why, she wondered, had being called Fenris bothered him so much? Many of the boys she'd known in high school would have relished the name, proud to be known by their peers as the mythological wolf.

Surely there was nothing connecting a Norse demon wolf, the wolf dog that howled outside Halfmoon House and Lycia's comment that *Cave Lupum*—Beware the Wolf—was the Volan motto.

After a while she realized the wind felt colder and was coming from a different direction. Dark clouds crept ominously up the sky.

"We may be in for some rain," she said. "The wind's changed." When he didn't react, she repeated, louder, "The wind's changed—it's shifted to the northwest."

Fenn whirled abruptly away from her, his back to the ocean, seeming surprised and confused to find no one there. "I thought someone spoke to me," he said.

Neita listened, then said, "I don't hear anything but the waves."

"It sounded as though the voice was directly in back of me, taunting me. Threatening me."

"Perhaps the cliffs triggered a memory."

"If that's true—" He didn't finish, but she refused to let him get away with evasion.

"Are you saying the truth might be that someone else was with you before you fell from that cliff in the mountains?" she demanded.

"I don't know. How can I know when I can't remember?"

"What did the voice say?"

"Something about a change," he said grimly.

"I told you the wind had shifted. I might have used the word 'change.'"

Fenn shook his head. "It wasn't your voice. And what was said had nothing to do with the wind. I suspect I heard the words in my mind and that they came from the blank in my memory." He half smiled. "Or else I'm one sandwich short of a picnic."

"Amnesia has nothing to do with going crazy, as I'm sure you know. You ought to feel encouraged that bits and pieces are coming back to you. It doesn't matter how they come."

"Patience isn't one of my virtues."

Neita smiled wryly. "I never would have guessed."

"You're right about the wind shifting," he said, glancing at the sky. "And those are rain clouds. Think we can outrun the storm?"

"We can try," she said doubtfully.

"The alternative is taking shelter in an old stone ruin that was once a Russian church. It's on our property, just behind those cypresses." He pointed south to where a dense row of the tall and narrow trees cut off any view of what was beyond them. "They aren't native trees. Uncle Theo thinks they must have been planted by the early Russian settlers. Volan's a Russian name, you know."

Intrigued, she opted for the ruins. Hurrying as fast as Fenn's recently healed leg would allow, they skirted the cypresses and crossed a weed- and sapling-infested meadow where large stones lay hidden beneath the thick growth. Neita didn't realize she was stepping over, on and around toppled ancient gravestones until she caught sight of barely legible chiseled letters on one of them.

"You didn't tell me a graveyard went with the church," she said.

"The Humboldt Historical Society has been after Uncle Theo for years, wanting to restore this cemetery," he said. " 'Over my dead body,' he always tells them. Theo does have a macabre sense of humor—his will leaves this part of the property, church and all, to the society."

As they approached the ruins, Neita saw that the church dome had fallen in. There didn't seem to be any roof, and one of the outer walls was entirely gone. She felt the first drops of rain on her face as she followed Fenn over tumbled stones until they entered the ruins. Three more or less intact walls had wooden planks angled overhead to form a crude roof.

"Weslin and I put the planks up years ago," Fenn said. "But the three of us didn't come here much—it was too dank and gloomy."

"It looks as though someone's been here recently, though," she said. She pointed to a plastic-covered black garment that hung neatly on a hanger hooked over a nail embedded in a stone. Curious, she took a closer look. "It seems to be a hooded cape."

"Don't touch it!" Dread edged his words.

Neita shifted her gaze to Fenn.

"I thought she was dead," he muttered as he stared at the cape. "She *has* to be dead."

About to ask who he meant, Neita realized that the cape must have reminded him of his Aunt Hensa. She started to reassure him, but the horror in his eyes made her realize words weren't sufficient.

Quickly crossing to him, she put a hand to either side of his face, forcing him to look at her rather than the cape. "Listen to me," she said firmly. "Your aunt Hensa has been dead for at least thirty years. That cape belongs to someone else."

He shuddered once, closing his eyes briefly. "Yes," he murmured. "Yes."

He didn't resist when, taking his arm, she turned him so his back was to the cape. Rain thrummed on the planks overhead and water dripped through the cracks between them. Unless she wanted them both to get soaked, they'd have to remain in this shelter until the rain let up.

"It wasn't only remembering Aunt Hensa that threw me," he said in a low tone. "I also have a gut feeling that cape is connected with my accident in the mountains." His voice rose. "Damn it, why can't I remember?"

"You will. In time."

"How long? A week? Next month? A year from now?"

Instead of making any attempt to answer the impossible, she asked a question of her own. "Do you have any idea why someone would hide a cape in here?"

"Maybe because afterward they need it to cover their nakedness."

She stared at him. "What on earth do you mean? After what?"

"Changing. Shifting."

The hair rose on her nape. She wanted to laugh, to accuse him of joking, but she couldn't. In this shadowy stone ruin with the rain pelting down outside, laughter was impossible.

"When we were kids at Halfmoon House," he said after a long silence, "Uncle Theo let us have the run of the place. Except for the underground stone vault we learned was hidden behind a steel door in the basement. That steel door was kept locked. We made up all sorts of stories about what was inside, but we never did get to see. We didn't even know when or if Uncle Theo ever went into the vault.

"One summer when we were all home from college, he showed us the vault, but that was the only time we ever passed through that locked door and along the entry corridor—a tunnel, actually—to the vault. The vault had a second locked steel door. Behind that door was an underground room. At the moment, that's what these ruins remind me of—the Volan vault."

Neita swallowed. "Did you ever learn what the vault was used for?"

"No. All I know is the doors remain locked to this day. After his injury, Uncle Theo could no longer get down the basement stairs to reach the vault, so if he ever did use it, he doesn't anymore. Why anyone would want to use the place is beyond me—it's nothing but a small stone room with no windows and no lighting and nothing whatsoever inside."

"Didn't you ask him about it? Once you were an adult, I mean."

Fenn shrugged. "He claims he kept it locked when we were young so we wouldn't be tempted to play there. 'I worried one of you might get locked in,' he once said. 'There's no mystery, none at all.' He had, he said, no idea why the Volans who built the house constructed the vault or what they might have used it for. What it reminds me of is a dungeon."

He glanced around the stone-walled ruins that sheltered them. "I hate to feel shut in. Even when we came here as kids, I never really liked this old church. Not the way Lycia did. She called it her special grotto. But none of us come here anymore."

Though he'd distracted her temporarily, Neita wasn't one to be easily sidetracked. "What did you mean about changing or shifting?"

"A morbid thought conceived in a gloomy place. It goes back to Aunt Hensa. The boy I was then believed in monsters, and I was convinced my murderous aunt turned into some kind of a ravening beast before she killed Donny, then shifted back to herself afterward. She was naked under the robe, I reasoned, because beasts don't wear clothes."

"A werewolf," Neita said, doing her best to keep her voice calm and level while trying to shrug off the chill his words brought. "So that's why you were upset when I mentioned that word earlier."

"You called me a werewolf."

"I did not! Besides, you know perfectly well it was merely a feeble effort at humor."

He took a step toward her. "It isn't a joke to me, Neita."

Another step brought him so close she had to look up to see his face. She resisted the impulse to edge backward. Why should she be afraid of Fenn?

He laid his palm against her cheek, sliding his hand down gently until it rested at her throat. She shivered, whether with anticipation or from nerves, she wasn't sure.

"You see, I have a problem," he murmured, his voice a sinister caress. "I can't be entirely certain I haven't inherited those same Volan genes."

"What genes?" she whispered.

"If you remember, my Aunt Hensa not only married a Volan, but was also distantly related to my uncle. She was a Volan herself. So it's possible she and I could carry the same taint."

"Taint?" Neita's voice was scarcely audible.

"Shapeshifting," he said, his fingers tightening at her throat enough to impede her breath. "Into a werewolf."

CHAPTER SEVEN

Fenn felt the pulsation of the blood in Neita's throat under his fingers, a rapid throbbing that matched the heavy drum of the rain on the makeshift roof. The sensation triggered a wildness in his own blood, and his desire flared, strong and violent as the wind that drove the rain through the crevices between the overhead planks.

Impelled by a passion he couldn't control, Fenn flung his arms around Neita and brought his mouth down hard on hers in a demanding, insistent kiss.

At first she resisted. Reluctantly summoning what scant willpower he had left, he was about to let her go when her lips opened invitingly under his. She relaxed against him, her fingers threading caressingly through his hair. Her increasingly ardent response delighted him.

No more, she'd said. Never again. But the infinitely arousing pressure of her body against his told him she couldn't withstand the irresistible tug of desire any more than he could. The attraction between them was too powerful to be denied.

Her spice-sweet scent beguiled him, he found her taste addictive, and her soft moans of pleasure thrilled him, urging him on. He wanted her more than he had ever imagined he could want a woman. Though these ruins were the last place he'd choose to make love with her, his passion was too overwhelming to fight.

"You've bewitched me," he murmured against her lips.

"No," she whispered. "It's you. You have an allure I can't resist." Still clinging to him, she shivered. "I'm afraid."

A chill ran through him. She had reason to be afraid of him.

"This is a bad place," she said, her voice still husky with desire. "Somehow evil. We shouldn't—"

She didn't finish, but she didn't have to. She'd said aloud what he already knew. It *was* an evil place; it always had been. To make love in these ruins would risk tainting what was between them. Tainting *her*.

It seemed to Fenn that he was tearing away part of himself when he let Neita go. "Not here," he said hoarsely. "But I don't promise to stop the next time."

Neita took a deep, ragged breath. She stepped back from him and crossed her arms. "There won't be a next time."

His smile was one-sided. "We both know there will be. Unless you leave Halfmoon House. Even then—" He broke off, appalled by the sudden realization that a darker motive lay hidden beneath his need for her.

There was no question that he desired her, but the pentagram he'd seen on her palm meant something far more sinister. The pentagram made him suspect he was other than human. If so, Neita had been chosen as his victim and might never be safe from him no matter where she went.

He noticed she was glancing around the shelter. "Do you hear a noise?" she asked.

He listened, finally hearing a faint mewing scarcely audible above the thrum of the rain. "Sounds like a cat," he said.

A search turned up a half-grown kitten, its fur drenched, huddled in a recess between the rocks. Neita picked up the tiny shivering animal, cuddling it to her breast.

"He needs to be dried off," she said.

Fenn shucked his sweatshirt, then pulled off the T-shirt he wore underneath and tossed it to Neita. By the time he was dressed again she was murmuring to the kitten while she toweled its striped yellow fur with his shirt.

"He's nothing but skin and bones," she said. "He must be starving."

"Let's hope he likes egg salad," Fenn said, reaching for the small nylon pack that carried the sandwiches Emily had made for them.

Neita found a relatively dry stone to sit on and held the kitten in her lap while Fenn offered it a morsel of egg salad, which he'd scraped off a sandwich with his forefinger. The kitten gulped it down and then attacked Fenn's finger hungrily.

"Hey, Tiger," he protested, jerking his finger away, "didn't you ever learn not to bite the hand that feeds you?" Fenn offered more and more of the egg mixture to the little cat until he could scrape no more off the sandwich. The kitten then ate the soggy bread except for the crusts.

After licking its drying fur smooth, the kitten curled up in Neita's lap and purred itself to sleep. By then the rain was diminishing, and soon it stopped altogether.

"We can't leave Tiger here to starve," she said. "I really would like to keep him."

"I agree we can't leave him. But there's a problem—Uncle Theo doesn't allow cats in the house."

"I forgot that Emily mentioned that the Volans were allergic to cats." She studied Fenn for a moment. "You don't seem to be suffering from any symptoms, though."

"I don't have any problem with cats. But Uncle Theo does and so do my cousins."

"If we can't bring Tiger to Halfmoon House, what shall we do with him?" she asked. "He needs a home."

Fenn thought for a few moments. "There's the Reynolds farm not too far away from Uncle Theo's, down on the flat. I went to high school with both Larry Reynolds and the girl he married, Marianne Tompkins. After we get back we can drive there and see if they'll adopt Tiger. If they will, maybe you can go and visit him. If they won't, we'll find some other solution." He plucked the kitten from her lap and nestled him in the crook of his arm. Tiger blinked his eyes and yawned.

"Your cousins have the same tawny eyes as he does," Neita observed as she stood up.

"Volan eyes," Fenn told her. "I inherited a different color from my mother."

"So I've noticed. Jade green eyes."

"Yours are as gray as fog," he told her, "and just as mysterious." Unable to resist the temptation to touch her, he leaned down and brushed her lips with his, savoring their sweetness. Then, despite his best intentions, he deepened the kiss.

If Tiger, caught between them, hadn't mewed a protest, Fenn would have pulled her into his arms. As it was, he drew back at the same time Neita did.

"I think we'd better leave," she warned him.

By the time they drove down the winding private road to the county road below, Tiger was fully awake and vociferously unhappy about being inside Fenn's car. He yowled despairingly and struggled to get away until Neita finally wrapped him into the damp T-shirt, with only his head free.

After they turned into the drive to the Reynolds farm, Neita kept expecting to be greeted by barking dogs. "I thought all farms had dogs," she said.

"This one does," he told her. "A couple of black-and-tan hounds, as I recall."

"Maybe they're tied up."

"And maybe not." His voice was somber.

She glanced at him, and his expression told her that he suspected what she did—that Zorn might not have been the only victim of the beast.

When they stopped near the white frame house, a toddler playing on the porch bumped his way down the steps on his rear and ran toward the car. A brown-haired woman rushed from the front door and hurried after him, reaching the boy just before he got to the car. By then Fenn and Neita had gotten out, Fenn leaving his door open.

"I swear this kid is going to turn my hair completely gray before I hit thirty-five," the woman said, trying to keep hold of the wriggling child. "He never stays put. Hello, Fenn," she added belatedly.

"Marianne, this is Neita," he said, "and we have a problem."

"Join the club," Marianne said as the boy broke free and began trying to climb into the car. "Robbie, stop that."

"Look what I've got, Robbie," Neita said, crouching to show the child the kitten. "Would you like to pet Tiger?"

Robbie toddled over to her and reached out his hand. Tiger licked his fingers and the boy squealed with delight. "Kitty," he said, patting the kitten's head with surprising gentleness.

"We were wondering if you'd like to adopt Tiger," Fenn said. "He needs a good home and my uncle happens to be allergic to cats."

"I suppose I could," Marianne said. "Robbie's going to really miss the dogs." She lowered her voice. "Something got the both of them last night. We've been hearing this awful howling, and then this morning Larry found the dogs in the woods over there." She nodded toward a pine grove to the south. "He buried what was left of them. Says he thinks a wolf's running loose."

Neita waited for Fenn to tell Marianne about Zorn, but all he said was, "Sorry to hear about your dogs."

Rising, Neita handed the kitten to Marianne. "Tiger seems healthy enough," she said, "even though he was half-starved when we found him."

Tiger tucked his head under Marianne's chin and began purring. She smiled and petted him. "He's a sweetheart, isn't he? I've always been partial to orange cats."

"Thanks for taking him," Fenn said. "Say hello to Larry for me."

Marianne nodded. "He'll be glad to know you're back on your feet again."

Neither Neita nor Fenn spoke after they said good-bye to Marianne and Robbie and drove up the hill toward Halfmoon House. They were almost to the garage when Fenn broke the silence. "Larry thinks it's a wolf, Emily favors a wolf dog. What do you think?"

She hesitated, then said honestly, "I don't know."

"Neither do I, not for certain." He maneuvered the car into its space in the garage and shut off the motor. "But whatever it is, the beast knows about me."

Neita stared at him. "Knows what about you?"

"That I might be—could be—what my Aunt Hensa was. It knows and it wants me to change. To be what it is."

Neita unbuckled her seat belt and turned to face him. "If you mean a werewolf, such things don't exist."

"Why are you so positive they don't?"

Neita blinked, beginning to realize the depth of what she saw as his unreasonable belief in a mythological creature. "I'm not denying that occasionally people think they're werewolves," she said carefully. "Medically, it's called lycanthropy. But as for actually shifting shape from human to beast—that's impossible."

"I wish I could be as sure as you are."

She laid her hand on his arm. "Fenn, believe me when I say you're not shadowed. There's no darkness within you. Even if I did believe in shape changers, I'd still be certain you weren't one."

He put his hand over hers. "I hope you're right. I hope the beast that howls when the moon is full is no more than some kind of vicious animal. I hope I'm wrong about Aunt Hensa, and that the underground vault of the Volans as well as the cape we found in the old ruins have no uncanny significance. I hope I hallucinated the pentagram I saw on your palm." His hand left hers. "I hope but I can't believe. If only I could remember...."

"Give yourself time."

"What happens if I run out of time before I regain my lost week of memory? That's what scares the hell out of me."

There was no denying she'd felt a sense of evil in the old ruins. But that had nothing to do with Fenn. "Have you discussed any of this with your doctor?"

He shook his head. "I don't intend to. You're the only one who knows, and I wouldn't have told you if I didn't worry about what might happen to you."

"Maybe you ought to—"

"No! Because of the amnesia, they had a shrink see me while I was still in the hospital. I didn't object then. I do now. A shrink can't help me, because I'm not crazy."

Neita bit her lip. While she agreed that Fenn wasn't psychotic, she couldn't be sure he wasn't suffering from a delusion that a psychiatrist *could* help him with. But there was no point in arguing with him at the moment, because he wouldn't listen.

After a late lunch, she persuaded Fenn to rest by telling him she intended to take a nap. It wasn't exactly untrue—only she planned to talk to his uncle Theo first.

When she went downstairs, Barnes agreed to take her message to Theo while she waited in the library. Soon afterward, her employer wheeled into the room, his hands still encased in gloves. He'd also been wearing gloves when he hired her, but she didn't find it unusual for someone using a wheelchair.

"If you're feeling well enough," she said without preamble, "I'd like to ask you a few questions about Fenn."

"I'm as well as I'll ever be." Theo's tone verged on testy. "You may ask all the questions you like, but I don't promise to answer each and every one."

"First of all," she began, "Fenn isn't happy about having a nurse."

Theo shrugged. "He needs one, whether he realizes it or not." His amber eyes narrowed as he gazed assessingly at her. "He needs you, specifically. I trust you've come to understand that by now."

"I agree that I might be able to help him," she said cautiously.

"Of course you can. I wouldn't have hired you otherwise."

"Have you ever discovered what happened to Jethro, the first nurse Fenn had?"

"He left without notice, taking his belongings. That's all I know." His tone suggested he didn't care to pursue the subject.

Neita tried to decide how much she could reveal about Fenn's werewolf obsession without violating a confidence. "Fenn has dreadful nightmares," she said at last. "And he's troubled about that creature howling at night. Especially since Zorn was killed."

Theo didn't respond immediately. Watching him, Neita thought he'd paled. "Troubled, is he?" Theo said at last. "How?"

"He seems to think the creature is calling to him."

Theo grimaced. "Watch him. Don't let him go out at night. The—beast won't be back until next month, when the moon is full." Theo paused, then added hastily, "At least, that was the pattern the month before, when all this started. I intend to take action when he—that is, it—returns."

"Action?" she repeated.

"In my own way, yes," he replied tersely.

Subject closed, she decided, so she changed tactics. "Why did you choose me as Fenn's nurse?"

"I think you know your own abilities. Let's say I sensed you have a special—talent, shall we call it?"

Taken aback, she stared at him. How could he sense anything special about her? She'd never been able to understand where the healing power that she was able to call up on occasion came from or why it sometimes worked and at other times failed her. The power had certainly failed disastrously for both of them when she'd tried to use it on Patrick.

"My grandmother was a *noita*," she admitted, then regretted telling him.

Theo nodded, accepting what she said with no surprise. Evidently he recognized the word. "Finns often have such talents," he said. "In this unbelieving day and age, unfortunately, few are trained to use their talent, and so it goes to waste." He pointed a gloved finger at her. "Don't waste yours."

Bringing herself firmly back to her concern for Fenn, she said, "The past troubles Fenn. He seems obsessed about his aunt Hensa."

"Damn the woman! She should have been drowned at birth like a defective pup. Always a troublemaker. I warned Leon not to marry her, but he wouldn't listen. Doomed them all, that's what she did. Little bitch!"

He swung his chair away from her, wheeled to the window, presenting his back to her. Neita wondered if he really saw anything outside the window or if he was, instead, examining the past.

She'd been screwing up her courage to ask if Hensa had actually killed Fenn's childhood friend but decided she'd better not since it seemed she'd already pushed Theo to his limit. And besides, maybe she'd be revealing too much of what Fenn had confided to her.

"I didn't mean to upset you," she said.

"Not your fault." He spoke without turning. When he didn't say anything else, she realized he expected her to leave.

"Thank you for answering my questions," she said. "I don't mean to pry, I'm merely trying to help Fenn, and I haven't enough information."

"You'll have to work blind. Like me. We're all blind until Fenn remembers."

She gazed at the back of the wheelchair and the broad shoulders and thick graying hair of the man sitting in it. Theo had told her all he was going to tell her. There'd been undercurrents she couldn't interpret in his words, and she promised herself that in the privacy of her room she'd review everything he'd said.

"I'm going now, Mr. Volan," she told him. Receiving no response, she let herself out of the library and went upstairs.

She'd left the connecting door ajar and was able to glance in at Fenn who was sprawled across his bed, eyes closed. She stood for a long moment looking at him, marveling at how boyishly innocent he looked when he slept. An upsurge of tenderness took her by surprise, making her turn abruptly away. She'd do well to keep in mind that Fenn wasn't a child, he was a man—a troubled and perhaps dangerous man.

In addition, she'd better not forget again that no matter how attractive she found him and no matter how desperately she longed to respond to his love-making, he was off-limits to her.

Acknowledging her own fatigue, Neita eased onto her own bed, intending to mull over what she'd learned from Theo. Instead, she fell asleep. And the nightmare came....

Strong hands gripped her shoulders, pushing—or were they pulling? She was trapped, half in, half out of the broken window, sharp shards of glass slicing into her. Screaming and struggling, she fought....

"Take it easy, Neita," a man's voice urged. "You're all right."

Was it the doctor?

Her eyes opened and she gazed blankly up at Fenn, who stood over her. Still caught in the dream's horror, she couldn't for a moment understand what he was doing in the hospital.

"You were dreaming," he said, his hands easing their grip on her shoulders, "and it must have been one hell of a nightmare because you screamed loud enough to wake me. When I rushed in to see what was wrong, you were thrashing around on the bed. Nothing I said seemed to get through to you, so I finally grabbed your shoulders and shook you."

Neita grasped one of his hands in both of hers, clinging to it as she slowly returned to reality. She was at Halfmoon House, not the hospital. She'd only dreamed she'd been struggling with Patrick to keep him from diving through the window he'd deliberately broken.

"At first I thought you were Patrick," she said, sitting up. "Then I thought you were the surgeon who..." Her words trailed off and she shook her head, releasing his hand. "I'm all right now."

Fenn sat on the bed. "Who's Patrick? What did he do to you that still gives you nightmares?"

She took a deep breath and looked away from him toward the window. Still daylight. She glanced at her watch.

"It's four o'clock," he said impatiently, "and I'm not moving until I find out who Patrick is."

"He's dead." Involuntarily, she cupped her hands over her lower abdomen. "I don't want to talk about him."

"He hurt you."

Without warning, she burst into tears, all but choking on great, gasping sobs. Fenn pulled her into his arms and she buried her face against his shoulder, crying for the first time over all she'd lost. She was barely aware of his hand stroking her back or his voice murmuring soothingly.

After a while her weeping eased and she freed herself. Fenn handed her tissues from the stand next to the bed, waiting until she wiped her face and composed herself before repeating, "What did Patrick do to you?"

Neita sighed and leaned against the headboard. "He was my patient. I thought I was helping him. I was wrong."

"That's not a complete enough answer. What happened?"

"Patrick broke the window of his tenth-floor hospital room with a chair and tried to dive through it. I tried to stop him. He—he almost took me with him. I would have fallen, too, if I hadn't gotten impaled on the fragments of glass left in the window." She hugged herself but couldn't prevent a shudder. "Patrick died in the fall—he was only eighteen. I was rushed to surgery and survived."

Fenn was silent for a long moment before leaning to her and running a caressing hand briefly along her cheek. "So we're both survivors," he said.

She nodded. "Except that I remember every detail of what happened."

"God, how I wish I did."

"Do you?" Her voice was bleak. "Take it from me, you might be better off never knowing."

CHAPTER EIGHT

Though Theo didn't dine with Fenn and Neita that evening, he joined them for coffee at the end of the meal. The conversation stayed away from the personal as they discussed recent films and the vagaries of California politics.

When she finally went to bed that night, Neita half expected to be roused by some unusual happening, but for the first time since her arrival, she slept through until morning. And so did Fenn.

In the days that followed, Theo appeared regularly for meals, so the three of them ate together. Theo had, she noticed, discarded the gloves. Each day she and Fenn hiked to one or another nearby elevation, hoping the height might trigger a clue to his lost memory. Though this didn't occur, Fenn's spirits did improve.

During her second week at Halfmoon House, they walked down to the Reynolds farm to see Tiger. Neita was pleased to note the kitten had already grown plumper—life at the farm obviously agreed with him.

"Robbie's crazy about Tiger," Marianne told them. "If the cat's not in sight, he searches all over the place and doesn't give up until he finds him. Luckily Tiger's good-natured and forgiving, because Robbie's pulled his tail more than once."

Good fortune had favored the cat—Tiger could afford to be forgiving. Actually, everything was going

well at Halfmoon House, too. No bad dreams plagued
Neita, and Fenn had no sleepwalking episodes.
Though she sensed an emotional tension building between them, much like storm clouds gathering, he
didn't so much as kiss her good-night.

The third week began as peacefully as the second.
Lycia and Weslin arrived early Friday evening, making Neita slightly uneasy. Would their presence disturb Fenn? She was relieved when it didn't seem to.

At dinner, the cousins reminisced about happy
childhood days, Uncle Theo joining in with a few
anecdotes of his own. Instead of excluding Neita as
she'd done before, Lycia made a point of making her
part of the group. After they'd eaten, Weslin proposed a game of chess to Fenn, and Theo announced
he'd kibitz.

Lycia bore Neita off to her room to show her the
Volan topaz pendant. "I usually keep it in my safety
deposit box," Lycia said as they climbed the stairs,
"but I wore it last night to one of those Bay Area mu-
seum benefits and didn't manage to get to the bank
today. So there was nothing to do but bring it along."

In Lycia's room, Neita watched her open a silver box
inlaid with gold and mother-of-pearl. Inside, glowing
against black velvet, rested a large teardrop topaz, one
of the largest gemstones Neita had ever seen.

"It's gorgeous," she said. "Absolutely magnifi-
cent." Glancing at Lycia, she added, "And it exactly
matches your eyes."

"The Volan topaz was chosen years ago to match
the Volan eyes," Lycia told her.

"The tawny eye color certainly seems to be a strongly inherited trait. Is Fenn the only one in the family who didn't get the golden eyes?"

Lycia shrugged. "I'm not sure. But he *is* a rarity." She smiled at Neita. "I can see *you* think he's something special."

Neita stiffened. "He's my patient."

"It wouldn't be the first time a nurse fell into bed with her patient."

"I don't believe in that kind of involvement with patients. It's not professional."

Lycia raised her eyebrows. "Are you serious?"

"I try to be."

"Ah, the truth emerges. You *are* attracted to Fenn, right? Don't bother to deny it—I can read your eyes. I certainly don't blame you—he's got everything any woman could want. Of course, he does have a few problems." Lycia sighed. "Is he still walking around in those middle-of-the-night trances?"

"Sleepwalking, you mean? Not lately."

"That's a relief. I've been so worried that something else might happen."

Neita frowned. "Something else?"

"I thought you knew that Fenn can't recall anything about the night Jethro disappeared. It's no wonder, because Fenn was wandering around in one of those strange trances—we couldn't find him for over an hour. And we never did find Jethro. We didn't admit it to each other, but I know we were all were worried to death that Fenn might have been responsible."

"Responsible for what?" Indignation laced Neita's words.

Lycia waved a hand. "Relax. I'm on Fenn's side as much as you are. After all, we're cousins. At the same time, I can't help wondering just what *did* happen to Jethro. You see, the guy was sort of a hunk and he and I got quite chummy while he was here. I don't believe he'd take off without letting me know. Or at least get in touch later. And he hasn't done that."

"Your uncle told me Jethro took his belongings with him," Neita said. "That would seem to indicate—"

Lycia shook her head. "Theo's wrong. Wes and I stored Jethro's things out of Fenn's sight to avoid upsetting him even more than he was already. The truth is, Jethro has simply dropped out of the world and I can't understand why. Unless—" She paused and shook her head. "No, I can't believe Fenn could have harmed him."

A chill shivered through Neita as she remembered Fenn, in one of his episodes of somnambulism, pinning her against the balcony rail under the mistaken notion she was his aunt Hensa. Was it possible—? She didn't want to think so.

"I really didn't mean to distress you," Lycia said. "Still, you had to know to protect yourself, in case I'm wrong and Fenn did dispose of Jethro without realizing what he was doing."

"He wouldn't."

"No, of course not!" Lycia put a touch too much emphasis on the words, betraying her own uncertainty. "Hey, that's enough of gloom and doom. Let's go down and join the guys."

As they descended the stairs, Lycia said, "The topaz wouldn't suit you at all. You're not the type. I wonder what sort of stone is right for you?"

Was she, Neita wondered, really conveying a warning that Fenn Volan wasn't suitable for someone like Neita Metsula?

"A moonstone, perhaps," Lycia mused. "Or even an opal. Not the fiery type, the other kind. Cool and pale, with hidden depths."

I'm reading too much into Lycia's words, Neita told herself firmly. I'm paying too much attention to what she says. About the topaz and about Fenn, too. He couldn't possibly have done away with Jethro.

"Yes, I believe you *do* have hidden depths," Lycia went on.

Glancing at her, Neita saw Lycia was gazing at her with narrowed, assessing eyes.

Deciding she'd had enough of Lycia's half-barbed remarks, Neita smiled thinly. "Why else would your uncle have hired me?" she asked.

They found Theo alone in the library. "Weslin claimed my kibitzing was costing him the game so he gave up," Theo said. "Actually, I think he was counting on Fenn's amnesia extending to chess and thus giving him a chance to win. Fenn's always been a better chess player than Weslin."

"Where are they?" Lycia asked.

"They went for a stroll around the grounds." He glanced at Neita. "It's safe enough at this time. Before dark, I mean."

Since it was already dusk, Neita had the feeling that his last few words were an afterthought and that "before dark" wasn't what he'd meant at all. Recalling him telling her that until the next full moon there'd be no more trouble with the beast that howled, she wondered if Theo had really meant Fenn and Weslin were safe because the moon, though waxing, was at least a week away from being full.

"I think I'll join them," Lycia said. "Coming, Neita?"

"Run along," Theo urged. "I'm going to retire."

When the women caught sight of the two men, Lycia hailed them and they paused. Zier, who'd been at Fenn's heels, trotted back and planted herself at Neita's side.

"It seems you've made a friend," Lycia commented as they approached the men.

Neita touched Zier's head. "I like dogs."

"Barnes told us about Zorn," Lycia said. "Too bad." Her tone was perfunctory.

Quite possibly Lycia didn't care for dogs, Neita told herself, excusing what seemed like callousness on the other woman's part.

Neita found herself walking with Weslin, with Fenn and Lycia dropping behind. Whether it was intentional on Lycia's or Weslin's part, she didn't know, but why should it matter? She dismissed her uneasiness and made up her mind to enjoy the stroll.

"There's something about you that intrigues me," Weslin said. "I can't put my finger on it, but it makes me want to find out more about you."

"There isn't much to tell."

"Everyone has secrets."

"Granted. But if told, they're no longer secrets."

Weslin chuckled. "I warn you I'm a wizard at ferreting out secrets."

"Perhaps I'm a wizard, period," she countered.

"I hadn't considered that." He sounded quite serious. "Maybe you do know about the shadow side of the mind, at that."

The shadow side of the mind? Did he mean the unconscious? The subconscious? The id?

"What terrors roam your shadow side?" Weslin asked.

"Whatever they may be, I've learned to suppress them," she said crisply, not caring for the turn the conversation had taken. "Nurses tend to be practical."

He moved closer so that his arm brushed her shoulder with each step they took. She wasn't exactly displeased—Weslin did appeal to her in some ways. At the same time, she didn't intend to encourage him. Before she could decide what to do, he clasped her hand in his.

Casual as the contact was, she didn't want it. She must have somehow communicated her feelings to Zier—perhaps by stiffening—because the dog growled, giving Neita the perfect excuse to withdraw her hand.

"I don't think Zier approves," she said lightly, "and I never argue with a Doberman. Which reminds me. Did you know Fenn and I found a kitten the other day?" She deliberately chattered on about taking Tiger to the Reynolds farm, finally saying, "I understand you and Lycia are allergic to cats."

"It's a Volan trait," Weslin said. So far he'd made no attempt to take her hand again.

"One that Fenn evidently doesn't share. Like his eyes being different."

"Fenn shares more than he realizes with us," Weslin said.

"Us?"

"The Volans, I mean. We're a unique family. But I'd far rather hear about you than talk about the Volans. What led you to become a nurse?"

"I wanted to learn more about healing." It was true. She'd known from the time she was seven that she had an ability none of her friends shared. By the time she was a teenager she'd learned to use this ability to help relieve pain in others.

"Why not a doctor, then?"

"Nurses are closer to patients. They have more direct contact with them." And direct contact was necessary for her to use her power to heal.

"What I don't understand," Weslin said, "is why Uncle Theo thinks Fenn still needs a nurse. No doubt Fenn appreciates your company—what red-blooded male wouldn't? But, hey, our cuz has come out of the doldrums and rejoined us. What's more, he hardly limps now. Does Theo imagine you can restore Fenn's missing memories?"

"I think Mr. Volan is aware no one but Fenn can do that."

"Do you have any idea how long you'll be at Half-moon House?"

"No." She really didn't know, though she was almost sure Theo intended her to stay until Fenn recovered from his amnesia.

Weslin glanced behind them and lowered his voice. "Uncle Theo must suspect the same thing I do and has hired you as a watchdog, much like Zier. Be careful, Neita. Be very careful. Fenn may seem to be recovering, but he's not in touch with his shadow side and that can be dangerous. Whatever you do, don't trust him.''

"First you tell me Fenn's recovered, then you warn me he hasn't. I'm not sure what you mean."

She'd tried to keep her tone neutral, but apparently she hadn't succeeded, because Weslin said, "Please don't be angry. I love Fenn dearly. I also know him well and that's why I'm concerned for you. These spells of his—" He paused. "I've said too much as it is, but here's one last warning. If you value your life, leave Halfmoon House before it's too late." Sincerity rang in his voice.

"Thank you for your concern." She knew the words were stiff, but it was the best she could manage. Despite her determination not to be alarmed by Weslin, what he and his sister had told her was disturbing.

It certainly was true that no one, not even Fenn, knew what lay buried in his mind amidst those lost memories.

After the four of them returned to the house, Fenn said he was tired and, without another word, mounted the stairs.

"It's been a pleasant evening," Neita told the twins, wondering if Fenn was all right or if something was bothering him. "I'll see you in the morning."

"What, you're deserting us, too?" Weslin asked. He turned to his sister. "And here I thought we were such fascinating company." He shrugged. "I guess we have no choice but to go into town and look up an old friend or two."

"How jolly." Lycia's tone was unenthusiastic.

"Good night," Neita said, leaving them standing in the entry discussing possibilities as she climbed the stairs. After all, she was here to take care of Fenn, not entertain his relatives.

When she tapped on the closed connecting door, Fenn muttered, "Come in."

She found him standing at his window with his back to her. "Anything I can do?" she asked.

"No." He didn't turn to face her.

He was shutting her out, she realized, the way he'd done when she first came. Why? She reviewed the evening. He'd been in good spirits through dinner. Then he'd gone into the library with his uncle and cousin, later taking a walk with Weslin. After she and Lycia had joined them, Fenn and Lycia had paired off. She didn't think Theo had said anything to upset Fenn—but Weslin—or more likely, Lycia—might have.

She hadn't yet decided what to do when Fenn growled, "I don't want company. Good night."

Neita returned to her room, though she did leave the door ajar. She sat in the rocker with the lights off for what seemed like hours, waiting to see what Fenn meant to do. She didn't get ready for bed until a series of rustlings and creakings from his room convinced her that he'd retired for the night.

Even then she lay awake listening. Much later she heard a car drive in—Weslin and Lycia returning, she assumed. After a time she got up to make certain Fenn really was in bed. Satisfied that he was, she relaxed, returned to her own bed and allowed herself to go to sleep.

Neita wasn't certain what woke her. All she knew when she sat up in the darkness, jerked abruptly from sleep, was that something was amiss. The lighted numbers on the clock showed her it was two-twenty. She rose, padded to the connecting door and found it shut. Alarmed, she shoved the door open and rushed into Fenn's room. His bed was empty. A quick search turned up nothing, not even his pajama bottoms. When she discovered the door to the hall ajar, she shook her head in dismay.

Was Fenn sleepwalking again? She feared he was.

Stopping in her room only long enough to grab her robe and slippers, she set off to look for him. Where, she asked herself, would he be likely to go? Unfortunately she had no idea. When she came into the entry and saw the front door wide open, her breath caught. Who else but a somnambulist would leave it open?

Slipping the lock so she'd be able to get back in, Neita left the house, closing the door behind her. The moon, just past half, gave scant light but enough, she felt, so she didn't need a flashlight. She got no farther than the drive when she froze in place, staring in fright at the animal loping toward her.

The beast! Terror gripped her by the throat. Theo had been wrong about the full moon.

Only when it was almost upon her did she recognize the Doberman. Her breath hissed out in relief as Zier trotted up to her. She crouched and hugged the big dog. "Zier," she asked softly, "where is Fenn? Find Fenn for me."

When she rose, the dog circled her, going nowhere, wriggling in delight at her presence. Neita shook her head. How could she convince Zier to lead her to

Fenn? Perhaps she should return to the house and rouse Weslin. As she tried to make up her mind what to do, Zier trotted away from her and along the drive, then stopped and looked back as though inviting her to follow.

Telling herself the dog must have seen Fenn leave the house, and fervently hoping Zier had decided to track him, Neita hurried toward the dog.

I'm safe enough, she assured herself nervously. Theo insists there's no danger from the beast unless the moon is full. Besides, Zier isn't acting threatened.

As she neared Zier, the Doberman, nose to the ground, trotted on. Trailing after her, Neita soon realized she was being led down the hill. Had Fenn come this far? She hesitated, and Zier, looking back, stopped and whined.

"Okay, I'm coming," Neita muttered. The dog was obviously following someone's trail and clearly wanted Neita with her. Since Zier was unlikely to be tracking a scent she didn't recognize, it must be Fenn's. But why had Fenn wandered so far from the house?

When the dog turned in at the Reynolds farm, Neita was relieved. Even in his trancelike sleep state, Fenn must have sensed a familiar place. Surely they'd find him soon. She began to worry again when Zier skirted the dark house and the outbuildings to plunge into the pine grove beyond Marianne's vegetable garden.

That's where Larry Reynolds had found what was left of their two dogs. Neita shivered, her pace lagging as she stepped into the gloom under the pines. Was it possible Zier could be following the beast's scent?

Again the Doberman paused to wait for her. "Stay!" Neita ordered, and Zier obediently sat down.

When she reached the dog, Neita ran her hands over Zier. The Doberman's hackles weren't raised and she didn't appear frightened or combative. Nevertheless, Neita couldn't force herself to go on into the dark pine grove. Even if she'd had the sense to bring her knife along, she wouldn't have found the courage.

Taking a deep breath, she called, "Fenn! Fenn, do you hear me?"

There was no answer, but she knew that didn't necessarily mean he wasn't within earshot. In a somnambulistic state, he might not react to his name. Zier whined again, eager to be moving. The sound reminded Neita that the barking of Zorn and Zier had roused Fenn before. But Dobermans were not given to barking for no good reason and she doubted she could find a way to make Zier bark.

"Fenn!" she called again.

"Mama!" a child's voice cried. "Mama, mama!"

The hair rose on Neita's nape. Had Fenn reverted to childhood in his trance? Listening, she heard the wailing of a frightened child and shook her head. Fenn couldn't possibly make that kind of sound. There was a real child lost in the grove.

Robbie?

She had to find him! Hooking a hand under Zier's collar, Neita urged the dog on, stumbling after her through the darkness, unable to see where either she or the dog was going. The child's sobbing grew louder and louder until at last Zier halted.

"Robbie?" Neita said, groping toward the sounds, hands outstretched. Her fingers brushed bare skin and she grabbed reflexively for what she'd touched, belatedly realizing at that height it couldn't possibly be Robbie.

She gasped and tried to step backward. She was too late. Tiny hands clutched at her and clung, refusing to let go. "Mama?" Robbie asked.

Confused and frightened, it took her a moment to understand that someone must be carrying Robbie. At the same moment, Robbie evidently realized she was not his mother, because he let her go and began to scream, high and piercingly. As Neita stumbled backwards, Zier started barking.

"Where the hell am I?" a man's voice demanded.

"Fenn!" Neita cried. "Oh, thank God. You've been sleepwalking again. I thought I'd never find you."

Some minutes later, with Fenn still holding the sniffling Robbie, they emerged from the pine grove. The Reynolds house was now lit up from top to bottom, and a man was shouting Robbie's name.

"Larry!" Fenn called to him. "I've got Robbie."

Once Robbie was safe in his father's arms, he fell into an exhausted sleep. "How the hell did you find him?" Larry asked Fenn as they started toward the farmhouse.

"The dog," Neita said, quickly putting together an explanation that she hoped would cover Fenn wearing only pajama bottoms and her being in nightclothes. "Zier apparently discovered Robbie in the grove and came back up the hill to alert us that something was wrong. She was so persistent that we finally followed her, never expecting she'd lead us so far. We had no idea Robbie was lost."

"That damn cat went missing sometime during the evening," Larry said. "Robbie was so upset we thought he'd never go to sleep. He must have gotten up in the night to look for the cat—we didn't hear him. Why Robbie went out the back door and all that way into the woods is beyond me—I don't think the cat would have gone there. What woke Marianne was the cat yowling to get in. That's when we discovered Robbie's bed was empty. Thank the Lord you found him before anything happened."

He smoothed his son's hair with a gentle hand. "I can't get those poor damn hounds out of my mind. I found them in the grove, you know."

"Marianne told us," Fenn said. "We lost Zorn the same night."

"So Wes said when he and Lycia dropped by earlier. If that beast returns, I'm damn well going to be ready for him."

Marianne, barefoot and wearing a nightshirt, met them by the vegetable garden. She took one look at Robbie dozing in his father's arms and began to cry. "Let me take him," she begged. "I need to hold him to be sure he's really all right."

As Larry handed over their son, he apparently took in Fenn's state of undress for the first time. "Hey, man," he said, "you're barefoot."

"Fenn lost his slippers while we were running after Zier," Neita said.

"I'll drive you two up the hill—it's the least I can do."

With Zier riding in the back of the pickup, they returned to Halfmoon House. There were no lights on inside; no one seemed to have noticed their absence.

Once upstairs, Neita insisted on Fenn washing his scratched and bruised feet.

He sat propped against the headboard of his bed afterward while she sat at his feet applying antibiotic cream to the worst of the cuts. "I don't think you'll get an infection," she said when she'd finished.

"Innovative, aren't you?" he said.

She knew he meant the lies she'd told Larry. "I could hardly say you found Robbie while you were sleepwalking."

"Did I?"

"I presume so."

"Which way was I headed when you found me in the pine grove?"

"Toward the farm."

"It was damned dark under the trees—how can you be sure?"

"You found Robbie in the woods and you were taking him home," she said firmly.

"You're being innovative again—too bad I can't buy it. Why not admit that neither of us know what I was doing? I could just as well have abducted Robbie and was taking him God knows where for some inexplicable reason. The last time I walked in my sleep I mistook you for Aunt Hensa. Maybe I was reliving the past and believed the boy was Donny."

"You certainly wouldn't have harmed him."

He gave her a twisted smile. "No? Why are you so sure? What if this time I believed that *I* was Aunt Hensa and mistook Robbie for my victim?"

CHAPTER NINE

Neita got to her feet, staring down at Fenn who was still propped against the headboard of his bed. "It makes more sense to me," she said, "that you found Robbie wandering in the woods and were bringing him home."

"If I don't know what I'm doing when I sleep-walk," Fenn argued, "will you explain how I knew who Robbie was and made the decision to rescue him?"

"I may not be able to explain it," she told him, "but I'm convinced that's what you were doing. You'd never harm a child. Never!"

He shook his head. "Go to bed, Neita. We're both too tired to think clearly."

Since he was right—she *was* exhausted—she decided to let it go until morning. Returning to her room, she fell into a sound sleep.

Neita roused to daylight and a complete absence of sound from the next room, even though the connecting door was ajar. It was past nine. Was he still sleeping? She doubted it. Springing from her bed, she padded over to look into Fenn's room. He wasn't there, but she noticed his pajama bottoms flung across the bed and her apprehension faded. Obviously he'd gotten dressed and no doubt had gone downstairs.

She found Fenn having breakfast in the morning room with Theo. "Weslin and Lycia aren't up yet?" she asked as she sat down and reached for the coffee carafe.

"Up and gone back to the city, so Barnes informs me," Theo said. "Like I did, apparently they missed the excitement during the night. Fenn's brought me up-to-date on what happened. I'm relieved everything turned out all right."

She glanced at Fenn, wondering exactly how he'd described the night's events to his uncle. He refused to meet her gaze.

Theo finished his coffee and set down the cup. "Fenn seems to think he won't be needing you any longer," he said.

Neita's heart sank. Fenn did need her. They were linked in a special way, with a bond that made her certain she was the only one who could help him. What did Theo intend to do? Keep her on despite Fenn's objection or say thank-you and goodbye? "I see," she managed to say.

"Did you know Fenn is planning a trip into Six Rivers up past Grouse Mountain?" Theo asked.

"I've never heard of Grouse Mountain," she said, concealing her surprise and trying not to feel resentful that Fenn hadn't mentioned the trip to her.

"Grouse Mountain's at the edge of Six Rivers National Forest," Theo explained. "The cliff Fenn apparently fell from is in the forest. He plans to revisit that cliff. Alone."

"No!" She couldn't hold back the protest. "No, not alone!"

Theo smiled. "My feeling exactly. So I've decided to go along."

Fenn stared at his uncle. "Impossible!"

"My dear boy, nothing is impossible. We'll use horses—I can still ride, you know. And I intend to bring Barnes and Neita with us. I'm sure they'll take excellent care of me."

"But," Fenn protested, "you're not well."

Theo shrugged. "My heart may be damaged but it's still working. When it does decide to stop, why should I care whether I'm in the mountains or at home? You can't dissuade me, so there's no use to try. I'll begin making plans immediately." He turned to Neita. "You don't mind a trip to the mountains, do you?"

She smiled, pleased that Theo meant to include her. "I'll enjoy going."

"Good! I'll just have a word with Barnes, and we'll be all set."

Fenn, admiration mixed with his very real annoyance, watched his uncle wheel away from the table. Theo had neatly outfoxed him. When he turned back to Neita, he found her glaring at him.

"You know better than to go back to that cliff alone," she snapped.

"Alone is the best way," he growled, shifting his annoyance to her. "Especially when I don't know what will happen once I get there."

"All the more reason to have someone along."

"You're like my uncle—you don't understand. I don't yet remember, but I'm beginning to be convinced I wasn't alone the first time, that someone or something was on that cliff with me. Something dangerous. What if the danger is waiting for my return?

Why should you and Theo and Barnes be forced to confront possible peril? Especially since I can't be sure some of the danger doesn't lie within me.''

Neita sighed. "Are we back to werewolves?"

He felt like shaking her. "You claim your grandmother was some kind of a Finnish wizard," he said. "Didn't she ever mention shapeshifters?"

"What if she did? Grandma Metsula was a true healer, but she also believed in old myths. Just because I've inherited a small part of her ability doesn't mean I have to embrace all her beliefs."

Neita sounded defensive, he thought, as though it might be a continual struggle for her not to accept all her grandmother had taught her. "What did Grandma Metsula have to say about werewolves?" he asked.

She took a sip of coffee before answering. "Not werewolves exactly. There's an old Finnish superstition about evil being able to survive death so that those who are evil in life come back from the dead as wolves. Though they can't shift from their animal forms, they possess the vicious cunning of the dead humans they once were and are almost impossible to kill."

"That sounds like a lethal combination."

Neita moved her shoulders uneasily. "It's merely a superstition."

"Or the remnant of an ancient truth. As the Volans are the remnants of an ancient Russian family. In old Russia, a shapeshifter was called *oborot*, meaning *one transformed*. Sometime in the 1800s, the word changed to *volkulaku*, more specifically referring to a wolf." He smiled thinly. "You'll note my family name begins with the same three letters."

She shook her head. "That doesn't mean there's any connection. And I, for one, have had enough of ancient days and ancient ways." Lifting the carafe, she poured herself a second cup of coffee. "Actually, as long as you don't go alone, I think it's a good idea to return to where you were injured. There's a possibility the surroundings might bring back the memory of what happened there."

"Uncle Theo is making damn certain I won't go alone. It's a wonder he didn't invite my cousins and make it a family expedition. Weslin and Lycia would have jumped at the chance. They've been at me for years to go camping with them, but something always interferes." Fenn frowned, a fragment of memory balancing on the edge of his mind. About camping? He couldn't quite grasp it and, when he tried harder, the fragment slipped away.

He became aware Neita had asked him a question. "Sorry, I didn't quite catch that," he said.

"I'm not from around here so I don't know much about this area," she said. "What exactly is Six Rivers?"

"It's not too far from Eureka, part of the coast range of mountains and pretty much wilderness. The Smith, Klamath, Trinity, Mad, Van Duzen and Eel Rivers run through there. Peaks and valleys, pines and firs, waterfalls, deer, bear, eagles—it's beautiful country."

"I've only been to the mountains once in my life," she said, her face bright with enthusiasm. "Six Rivers sounds wonderful."

Watching her, he felt the tie between them tighten. As though she felt it, too, she set down her cup, and her gaze met his. Her cool gray eyes began to glow with warmth, fueling the desire already heating him. If the table wasn't separating them, she'd be in his arms. He'd never be able to break the link between them—never. Why had he thought he could?

He rose, his gaze still holding hers. She got to her feet. He skirted the table and took her hand, leading her through the French doors opening onto the terrace. When they stood face-to-face on the sun-warmed bricks, he leaned to her, his lips brushing hers in a tentative, coaxing kiss.

Her lips quivered under his, opening as she offered the sweetness of her mouth to him. He deepened the kiss, still not touching her otherwise, relishing her eager response. The bond tugged at both of them, he knew, a demanding, irresistible force drawing them together against his better judgment. Against hers, too, as she'd already told him.

For her own safety he ought to send her away, far away from him. He kept trying and failing. The truth was he wanted to keep her with him, near enough to see and hear, close enough to touch. To make love with. To cherish.

At the same time he knew how dangerous it might be. For her.

Exerting willpower he wasn't aware he possessed, Fenn drew back. "You know how much I want you," he said hoarsely, "but . . ." He let the words trail off.

She touched his lips with her fingers. "But you're haunted by what you can't remember," she said softly.

Zier bounded onto the terrace to greet them, shattering the moment. "Hey, you ought to be in your pen," Fenn told the dog as he fondled her ears.

"I'm letting her run free during the day now." Theo spoke from the open French door behind them, making Fenn wonder how long his uncle had been there. "And I've told Emily to keep Zier in the house with her at night while we're in the mountains. It's safer."

Safer for Emily or for Zier? Fenn asked himself. Maybe for both.

"I think it would be a good idea for you two to drop in on the Reynolds this morning," Theo said. "Before we leave for Six Rivers, I'd like to be certain their little boy is all right after his horrendous experience."

"I'm not so sure they'll want to see me," Fenn said.

"Believe me, they will."

"I agree we should check on Robbie," Neita said, siding with his uncle. "And Tiger, too, for that matter."

Theo nodded. "Ah, yes, the cat. Presumably the missing cat was what lured Robbie from the house— am I right?"

"That's what we were told," Neita said.

"Clever," Theo commented.

Fenn frowned. "Why clever?"

"I meant the child must be unusually clever to trail the cat into the night woods at such a young age."

Fenn had the distinct impression his uncle had really meant something else entirely, but he didn't pursue it.

"Take the car," Theo advised. "If everything goes well, we should be leaving on our trip by tomorrow, and I intend to see that Neita is equipped for wilderness travel. Go on in to Eureka and buy her what she needs."

Fenn nodded. As usual, Theo was on top of things.

* * *

When they arrived at the Reynolds farm, Marianne was sitting on the front porch steps watching Robbie play nearby in a pile of sand with a toy dump truck. Tiger, stretched out on a low limb of an old apple tree, blinked lazily as they approached.

"We wondered how Robbie was," Neita said, sitting next to Marianne.

"Better than I am," Marianne told her. "He seems none the worse, but I'm a nervous wreck. I can't bear to let him out of my sight for a second."

Fenn hunched down beside the boy. Robbie looked at him solemnly for a moment before saying, "You."

"Yeah, it's me all right," Fenn agreed. "My name's Fenn."

Robbie glanced around. "Lady?" he asked.

"The lady's over there on the steps with your mama."

Robbie peered at Neita and shook his head. "'Nother lady."

"Neita's the only lady with me," Fenn told him.

"Kitty," Robbie said, pointing at the tree. "Tigah."

"Right—Tiger's the kitty's name."

"'Nother lady," Robbie repeated. "Tigah."

Fenn could make no sense of this.

Losing interest in the conversation, Robbie resumed playing with the truck, making appropriate engine noises. Fenn rose and strolled over to the steps.

"I heard what Robbie told you," Marianne said. "He's repeated the same words to Larry and me. 'Lady,' and then 'Tiger.' It reminds me of that story we read in high school about the lady and the tiger—

wasn't there something about choosing between two doors?''

Choosing between life and death, as Fenn recalled the story. "Apparently Robbie doesn't mean Neita," he said, "but another lady, whoever she may be."

"Lycia was here yesterday evening, wasn't she?" Neita said. "Could Robbie mean her?"

Marianne blinked. "You may be right," she said slowly. "Robbie could be remembering how, for some reason, Tiger panicked when Wes and Lycia came in. The cat took off like a rifle shot for the kitchen, with Robbie in hot pursuit. When Robbie didn't find Tiger, I assumed the cat had crept behind the refrigerator, his favorite hiding place. Come to think of it, though, I never did see the cat after that. Not until after midnight when he cried at the back door to come in and we discovered Robbie was missing."

"Is it possible for Tiger to leave the house without someone opening a door for him?" Neita asked.

"Not as far as I know. I didn't notice at the time, but maybe he slipped out when Wes and Lycia left. I'll bet that's what happened." She shook her head ruefully. "With the logic of an almost two-year-old, Robbie might blame Lycia for Tiger's disappearance. Though he *did* seem to like her. Ordinarily he doesn't take to strangers, but he willingly sat on her lap while they played a game Lycia called Secrets, involving a lot of whispering to each other. In my opinion, it's high time she thought about having a child of her own."

Fenn knew Lycia couldn't, but that was none of Marianne's affair. From his observation, his cousin had always seemed to find children more annoying than endearing, but then, perhaps she'd changed.

"I was too upset last night to thank you properly," Marianne said. "It was a miracle, your Doberman rousing you and you finding Robbie. If there's ever anything we can do for either of you, you've only to ask."

"The credit goes to Zier and Neita," Fenn said, feeling acutely uncomfortable. "Neita, we really should be going," he added.

Neita rose from the step, saying, "We're so glad Robbie's okay."

As the two of them walked to the car, Fenn reran in his mind Marianne's account of the cat's disappearance. Something she'd said had disturbed him. What? He couldn't pin it down.

"That's a truly ferocious scowl," Neita said when he started the car.

"I have a hunch I missed an important detail," he muttered.

She didn't speak again until they were on their way into town. "I'm the one who should be scowling," she told him.

He gave up trying to figure out what was nagging at him and focused his attention on her. "I'll admit I should have talked to you before I spoke to Uncle Theo. But when I looked in this morning, you were sleeping so peacefully..." He paused, reminded of how he'd had to fight his urge to kiss her awake. "But it couldn't have come as any surprise that I want you to leave," he said. "It's for your own good, as I've told you enough times."

"I've thought seriously about going," she admitted.

Instead of the satisfaction he ought to feel, apprehension stabbed him.

"We'll discuss what I should do after we return from this trip to the mountains," she went on. "By then you may have your memories back."

Though she didn't say it, *and therefore won't need me* was implicit. Fenn took a deep breath, startled by how troubled he was by the threat of losing her. He wanted her safely away from him and yet he couldn't bear the thought of having her gone.

"What did Lycia say to you when you were walking with her last evening?" Neita asked, the abrupt change of subject jolting him from his unhappy reverie.

"My sleepwalking," he muttered.

"What about it?"

"Why the devil do you need to know?"

"Because whatever she said upset you and might well have triggered the somnambulistic episode later. I can guess what Lycia said because she made a point of discussing what she called your 'trances' with me while you were playing chess with Weslin. She claimed you were sleepwalking when Jethro vanished into the blue and hinted at a connection between the two."

"I *was* sleepwalking. Which is why I don't know where the hell Jethro went. Nor do I know whether or not I had anything to do with his departure."

"So Lycia wasn't telling you anything new?"

He shook his head. "No, except she confessed she and Weslin hid Jethro's clothes to protect me. I got a strong impression she might be about to reach the same conclusion I've already come to."

Neita shot him a disgusted look. "I suppose you mean your cousin is beginning to suspect you're some kind of a shapeshifter."

"Don't forget Aunt Hensa was her mother," Fenn said. "It's true Lycia was even younger than I when all our parents died in the fire, but she couldn't have been completely unaware of what Hensa was. Ask yourself this—if I am, as you'd like to believe, completely innocent where Jethro's concerned, then where in God's name is he? What would compel an ordinary, law-abiding man like Jethro to vanish like smoke in the wind?"

"I don't know. But—"

He cut her off. "I'll tell you, then. Nothing. Jethro didn't disappear of his own accord. Someone else was involved. Or some*thing*."

"Lycia should have had enough sense to keep her mouth shut." Neita spoke heatedly. "She must have realized she'd upset you."

"Lycia was trying to do me a favor, to warn me."

Neita set her chin stubbornly. The hell Lycia was! Fenn had a blind spot where his beautiful cousin was concerned. For some reason Lycia had wanted to rattle him, and she'd done just that. Fenn had been rapidly improving, with no more somnambulism, until Lycia's little talk with him. Was she the type of woman who got a charge out of needling others—especially relatives? If so, this verged on vindictiveness. Or was there some other reason, one so covert it couldn't even be guessed at? In any case, Neita couldn't easily forgive her.

Realizing nothing would be accomplished by airing her opinion of Lycia, Neita concentrated on calming herself. Glancing at Fenn, she sighed inwardly when she saw the grim set of his jaw. How could she lighten his dark mood? And her own, for that matter.

By the time a truly zany idea struck her, they'd reached the outskirts of town. "What would you do," she asked, "if I grabbed the wheel, forced the car onto the shoulder, killed the motor, dragged you into the ditch and began making mad, passionate love to you?"

For a second or two, he stared blankly at her. Then a smile curved his lips. "I don't know," he admitted, "but I'd enjoy finding out. Why don't we try it and see what happens?"

Though a trifle taken aback by his challenge—she hadn't really expected that kind of response—she concealed her feelings.

If you think you can call my bluff, she told him silently, you're way off base.

Choosing the moment carefully—no oncoming cars and a conveniently wide space past the shoulder of the road—she reached over, grasped the steering wheel and turned it to the right, swerving the car off onto the shoulder. He immediately took his foot off the accelerator. They bumped over several rough spots before the car slowed enough for her to stomp on the brake and cut the motor. The car came to rest near a stand of young willows.

She undid her seat belt. As she released his, she murmured, "I've altered my plans."

She then leaned over, pushed the button that lowered his seat back, and when the back—and Fenn—lay almost flat, she wriggled closer and eased herself down until she rested against him.

Up until the moment her lips met his, she'd meant it as a joke, but when he wrapped his arms around her, the kiss turned from tepid to hot, and suddenly the idea of making mad, passionate love was no joke, but utter, wonderful reality.

Time and place faded, vanishing as Fenn molded her against the hard length of his body. She could feel his physical need for her—and more. Because of the strange bond between them, she could also sense his desire, intense and acute as her own, a throbbing, aching demand that pulsed through her mind and body.

He is the one, a voice within her whispered. *Fenn is the one and only man you will ever love with all of your being.*

Why not seize the moment? Why not make love with him here and now? Balanced as they were on the edge of dreadful, unknown peril, this might prove to be their only chance to experience the full measure of their bonding.

Nothing existed for her except Fenn—his caressing hands, his lips, his passion. She wanted more of him, wanted all he could give her while at the same time offering him her own passionate love. With a thrill, she realized he felt the same desperate yearning.

When he suddenly thrust her away from him and struggled to sit up, she moaned in protest, not understanding. And then she heard the tapping on the driver's window. Startled, she stared into a man's amused face on the other side of the glass, belatedly noticing he wore a uniform.

As Neita hastily rearranged her clothing, Fenn raised the back of his seat and eased the window open. "Hello, Pete," he said gruffly.

"I recognized your car," the Eureka policeman said to him. "Figured you might need some help." His grin broadened. "Sorry. Should have remembered good old Fenris never fumbled a pass." He nodded to Neita, turned and walked back to his patrol car.

Fenn looked at her ruefully. "Pete always did have lousy timing."

Her chagrin faded and she began to laugh. "Such is the price of fame," she told him.

As he joined in her laughter, her heart lifted. They might both be frustrated but at least his dark mood had lightened.

CHAPTER TEN

The Volan pack train was well into the mountains when Fenn ordered a halt at noon to rest the horses as well as the humans. As Neita dismounted, she could feel her muscles beginning to protest—she hadn't ridden in years. Concerned about Theo's comfort, she hurried to unroll and spread a blanket on the ground for him while Barnes and Fenn unhooked the special harness holding him in place and lifted him off his horse.

Theo settled under a fir on the blanket, propped up on two rolled sleeping bags, and began issuing orders. "I need something hot. That dehydrated soup will do. Fenn, you start the fire and boil some water. Barnes, get the rest of the lunch ready. Neita, come sit beside me."

At first Theo spoke to her in his normal tone. "I realize Fenn's going to use the camp stove to make the soup. Why not, since it's easier than scrounging for firewood? But, like his cousins, he *is* a skilled woodsman. I taught the three of them myself. Did you know one way to estimate wilderness skill is to see if the person can light a fire, no matter what the weather, with one match? Of course, nowadays there are dozens of supposedly infallible lighting gadgets." He paused and glanced around.

Lowering his voice, he said, "While I might be able to make it all the way to the cliff, I'm not sure I could stand the return trip, so it's best for me not to take the chance. After lunch I'll announce I'm not going on. Fenn will insist on you returning with me, but you must continue on with him. He can't be left alone."

At the moment she was more worried about Theo. "Are you having chest pain?" she asked, reaching for his wrist to check his pulse.

He jerked his arm away. "Don't fuss over me. I assure you I'm not going to drop dead on the spot. We only have a few minutes to talk, so listen carefully. Don't allow Fenn to stay in the mountains any longer than planned—today, tomorrow, and the trip back the following day, at the most. You both *must* return to my house before the full moon. Nothing must stop you. Do you understand?"

If he meant did she understand *why,* Neita didn't. But she knew that wasn't what Theo was asking. "I understand," she said, "that nothing must keep us from being back at Halfmoon House by the day after tomorrow."

"Are you armed?"

Unprepared for such a question, Neita stared at him for a long moment before answering. "Armed? Like with a gun? No."

"I meant *any* weapon."

Involuntarily, she touched her right hip. Her Finnish knife, in its special sheath, was fastened inside the pocket of her riding pants. "I have a knife," she admitted.

"Show me."

Neita slid her hand into her pocket and eased the small dagger from the sheath. She didn't offer to hand it to Theo because she preferred not to have anyone but herself touch the dagger.

He peered at the hilt, studying the incised runes. "Old and beautiful," he commented. "Tiny but lethal-looking. I notice the hilt is silver, but I imagine the blade must be steel?"

She shook her head. "The knife is all silver." Though she didn't intend to repeat it to Theo, Grandma Metsula had recited a Finnish rhyme to explain why. Roughly translated the couplet went:

A silver dagger keeps away,
What steel and iron cannot slay.

"I might have expected a *noita* blade to be silver," Theo said as Neita slid the knife back into its hidden sheath. "Excellent. What's that all but untranslatable word the Finns use to describe the inner spirit—*sisu?* Your *sisu* shines through so clearly I could sense it the moment I first laid eyes on you. That's how I knew you were the right one for Fenn."

Though Neita wasn't sure, she thought Theo was telling her that he could sense darkness and light in certain people in the same way she could. But no matter how much *sisu* he believed she had, it gave her chills to imagine what he might expect her to fend off with her silver dagger.

"I hope the occasion will never arise where you'll be forced to use the dagger," he said.

She found his words small comfort.

Theo grasped her hand, holding it firmly in his for a long moment, and something intangible—was it a kind of power?—seemed to pass from him to her before he released her hand.

"Take over what Barnes is doing and send him to me," Theo ordered.

Barnes had finished laying out the food for lunch and was by the camp stove, handing a packet of dried vegetable soup to Fenn. When she gave him Theo's message, Barnes hurried away. Neita stayed where she was, staring at the pan on top of the stove and feeling that her mind was seething and bubbling like the simmering water. She willed herself to be calm.

"Is Uncle Theo all right?" Fenn asked as he poured the dried packet of soup into the water and then stirred the mixture.

Neita chose her words carefully. "He's in no immediate danger of collapsing, but he did admit to feeling tired."

"I knew he shouldn't have come," Fenn muttered. "Do you think he ought to go on?"

Neita shrugged. "Your uncle seems to make his own decisions, no matter what others may think is best."

Fenn scowled. "We'll see about that."

When the soup was ready, she and Fenn joined Theo. Barnes was over by the packhorses, and when Fenn shouted for him to come and eat, Barnes called back, "I'll be there in a minute."

"We'll start without him," Theo said. "I need that hot soup to revive me."

Neita was through eating her soup by the time Barnes finally joined them. As though his arrival had been a signal, Theo placed his half-finished container of soup on the ground, muttering, "That's all I want." Then, fixing his gaze on Fenn, Theo sighed and said,

"I should have listened to you, my boy. I'm getting too old and feeble for pack trips into the mountains. I thought maybe I'd feel better after I ate, but I was wrong. The truth is, I'm nearly exhausted."

"Then you damn well are going to turn back here and now and go home," Fenn told him. "You and Barnes and Neita. I'll go on alone."

Theo shook his head. "I won't hear of it!"

"You have no choice." Fenn spoke firmly.

"It's true *I* don't," Theo admitted. "And, of course, I'll need Barnes's strong arm to help me. But I have no need of a nurse. Neita won't return with me—she'll go on with you."

"I don't—"

Theo cut Fenn off. "I won't hear of you riding to that place alone. Neita goes with you. Otherwise, I'll have to try to pull myself together enough for us all to continue to the cliff."

Though Fenn went on protesting, it was clear to Neita that Theo had won. He and Barnes would return home while she and Fenn rode to the cliff.

"I won't listen to another word," Theo finally announced. "Barnes has already rearranged the gear so that you can take one packhorse with what you'll need and we'll bring the rest of the things back with us on the second packhorse." He turned away from Fenn. "Barnes, I'm ready to get aboard that old dun again and make tracks for the lowlands."

In the end, Theo and Barnes rode off with one packhorse, leaving Neita and Fenn behind.

"My uncle is sly as a fox," Fenn grumbled to Neita as he stowed the camp stove while she cleaned up the utensils they'd used. "I swear he had this planned from the moment I mentioned returning to the cliff."

"Do you really think so?"

"What else? He knew I'd never agree to bringing you along with me, so he thought up his devious little plot to force my hand by making you just one of the crowd. Then he waited until the four of us were half-way there before producing his clever ultimatum that put me between a rock and a hard place."

"You have a talent for making me feel really wanted," she said coolly.

Fenn finished tying the camp stove onto the pack-horse before striding over to her. Clamping his hands onto her shoulders and staring into her eyes, he said, "You know damn well how much I want you. But this is a trip I should be making alone." He shook his head, released her and turned back to the horses. "Time to ride, as they say in the old Westerns."

"What they say is, 'Time to ride, partner,'" she corrected.

His mouth quirked into a reluctant grin. "You don't have it quite right—it's 'ole pard.'"

"*Kemo sabe,* would-be Lone Ranger," she said airily, and mounted her pinto.

In the late afternoon, Fenn reined in his sorrel and dismounted by a stream that meandered through a small glade. "We'll camp here for the night," he said. "The cliff's an easy hike from this spot."

"Do you remember this meadow?" she asked.

He shook his head. "I'm going by Uncle Theo's detailed forest-service map."

Neita slid from her horse, wincing at muscle twinges. But as she gazed at the giant firs surrounding the charming little meadow, she drew in her breath, forgetting minor aches and pains, awed by the beauty around her. Impulsively she flung out her hands as though to embrace all she saw.

"I'm so glad to be here!" she cried.

"Let's hope you keep feeling that way." Fenn's tone was dark.

Somewhat deflated, she began to help him unload the packhorse. After they'd rubbed all three horses down and hobbled them, Fenn chose a spot away from the stream and near the trees and began setting up a tent—the small one, she noticed. He refused her help.

"You can help me gather firewood when I'm done," he said.

"I could do that now."

"Wait. You've admitted you're a tyro camper, and I'm particular about the kind of wood I use for my fires. What you could do is take a look around the edge of the meadow for a deadfall—a downed tree. But don't go into the forest without me—it's easier than you think to get lost in the woods."

Get lost? What kind of idiot does he think I am? she grumbled to herself as she walked toward the trees.

"If you do get lost," he called to her, "don't keep wandering around. Stop and keep shouting my name so I can find you."

Did he actually believe she was going to plunge into the darkness under those big trees and keep going until she didn't know where she was? On the trail she hadn't been intimidated by the vastness of the forest nor its perpetual gloom, and she wasn't now, but that didn't mean she intended to venture very far on her own.

She'd gone halfway around the irregular circle of the meadow when she spotted what Fenn had called a deadfall. She called to him, reporting her find, then, since the fallen fir was only a short way into the woods, she stepped under the canopy of needled branches, wondering whether a catastrophe of nature, old age or disease had felled the huge tree.

There'd been birds in the meadow but there were none here beneath the trees, where slim arrows of sunlight failed to lighten the prevailing darkness. Neita took a deep breath, inhaling the forest odor of conifers and of brown needles decaying under her feet, combined with the freshness of the mountain air. She walked a few more yards into the forest, her heart quickening in response to her surroundings.

Something within her was attuned to this place, to the aromatic scent, to the towering trees, to the hushed music of the wind as it caressed the branches, even to the deep shadows around her. Lines she recalled from her childhood rose to her tongue:

> "Widespread the Northland's dusky forests,
> Mysterious, breeding ancient savage dreams;
> Here dwells the great lord of the forest,
> Within the secret gloom his magic reigns...."

She paused, a frisson of fear snaking along her spine, wishing she hadn't spoken those words from the Finnish *Kalevala*. It was almost as though in reciting them she'd evoked some savage forest spirit that was even now approaching, slipping soundlessly between the trees. Powerless to move, she waited. Was the wind in the branches whispering her name? Summoning her? The hair on her nape rose as she strained to hear.

"Neita!"

She gasped.

"Damn it, I told you not to wander off," Fenn called. "Where the hell are you?"

Her trance broken, she turned toward the sound of his voice. To her shock, she couldn't see the meadow. Somehow she'd gone farther into the woods than she'd meant to.

"Fenn!" she cried. "I'm over here."

"Stay put and keep calling. I'll find you."

By the time he appeared, embarrassment mingled with her relief. How could she have been so careless? And after he'd warned her. Without a word, Fenn grasped her hand, leading her between the trees.

"I feel like a fool," she said. "I don't know what came over me."

"Don't apologize. Deep woods like these have a mystic appeal for me, too—it's as though something lures you on. When I was younger I had my own turn at getting lost."

Mystic appeal or not, she was glad when they came out from under the trees into the meadow, lit by the lowering sun.

"You look through the supplies and choose what we'll have for supper," he said, "while I gather firewood."

She didn't argue, aware he was taking no chances on her wandering off again.

After the fire was lit—with one match—Fenn announced he'd do the cooking. "I've been waited on so much in the past few months," he told her, "that it's a pleasure to be able to do something for another person." His smile was warm. "Especially for you."

Neita watched Fenn remove the food for their supper, then followed him as he strode across the meadow carrying the pack with the remaining food, a long forked stick, a coil of rope and a fist-sized stone. He stopped at a tree at the edge of the meadow, far from the tent, and, weighting one end of the rope with the stone, tossed it over a high branch some feet away from the trunk.

When the rope was securely looped over the branch, he tied the pack to one end and removed the small stone from the other. After hefting several larger stones, he found one that suited him. "The stone has to match the weight of the pack," he told her.

Before tying the bigger stone to the rope, he pulled on the free end so that the food pack rose until it almost reached the branch. "Hold the rope," he ordered.

After she obeyed, he wrapped many turns of the rope around the stone, finally tying it. She released her hold. Taking the stick, he pushed the stone up into the air and, as he did, the food bag lowered. When both bag and stone were at the same height, about fifteen feet off the ground, he stopped, stepped back and eyed the result.

"No bear's going to reach that," he said with satisfaction.

"Bear?" she repeated, glancing around a bit nervously.

"We're on their turf now," he said casually. "Bears don't usually bother humans but they're often interested in the food campers carry. That's why experienced campers keep no food in their tents or near the horses. And it's why I've cached the food bag so far from the tent.''

For some reason, she hadn't thought about bears, even though she knew there were wild animals in these mountains. Her silver dagger would be of no use against a bear. But Theo, she was certain, had not been referring to bears when he asked if she was armed.

What *had* he meant?

"Do you carry a gun when you camp?" she asked.

Fenn shook his head. "Never have. And I've never needed one."

Would it have made a difference if he'd had a gun the last time he was in these mountains? she wondered. Or was his fall from the cliff merely an accident? Apparently neither Fenn nor his uncle believed the fall had been accidental. Recalling Fenn's nightmares and somnambulism, she was inclined to agree with them.

She'd deliberately kept her thoughts away from the night's sleeping arrangements. Originally, Fenn, Theo and Barnes were to share the large tent and she'd have been alone in the small one. But evidently the large tent had been on the packhorse Theo and Barnes took with them. Had that been deliberate on Theo's part? There was barely room for one person in the small tent—surely Theo couldn't have planned for her to share it with Fenn.

Once she began thinking about the coming night, she couldn't divert her mind into any other channel. The anticipation of their enforced intimacy made her acutely aware of Fenn's every nuance of expression. What was on *his* mind?

When they'd eaten, cleaned up and were walking back from the creek toward the dying fire, Neita looked up at the late evening sky, already dark enough to show the glimmer of the stars and the pale glow of the newly risen moon. Theo's warning about the full moon echoed in her head and she shivered, huddling into her jacket.

Fenn put his arm over her shoulders, drawing her closer to him. "It gets cold in the mountains this time of the year," he said.

As they continued on toward the fire, she asked, "Are you still annoyed because you were forced to bring me on this trip?"

He didn't answer until they halted by the fire. His gaze was intent as he murmured, "What do you think?"

The glow of the last flickering flames illuminated his face, reflecting in his eyes and making him appear both mysterious and dangerous. And seductive. Her heart speeded in response.

"You don't look unhappy," she said softly.

He glanced toward the tent, then ran his forefinger across her lips. "A gentleman might offer to sleep under the stars," he said.

"I suppose he might." She was amazed her voice didn't reveal her breathlessness.

"Since, among other things, I can't remember whether I ever was a gentleman or not, I'll opt for not." He brushed his mouth over hers, caressing her lips with the tip of his tongue. "Did you ever notice how things taste better in the mountains?" he whispered.

She was already too bemused to tell him he tasted wonderful under any circumstances.

Moments later he unfastened the tent flap and followed her inside the tiny enclosure where he turned on a battery lantern. The first thing she saw was that he'd already opened their sleeping bags and zipped them together.

She raised her eyebrows and he grinned at her, both of them kneeling on the sleeping bags as they faced one another.

"Would you believe I zipped the bags together because we have more room this way?" he asked.

She shook her head.

"How about it's so we'll be warmer during this cold mountain night?" he said.

"How about, it's because you're Mr. Confident personified?"

He gave her a pained look. "You're condemning me without a trial. Before we left the house I told you I didn't need a nurse any longer—remember? So, since I'm not your patient now, I figured I might be able to persuade you to get involved with me. Once we arrived, I decided that we might as well be comfortable while we discuss the pros and cons of the situation."

"Intimately comfortable, I think you mean."

"Isn't that the best kind of comfortable?" He unzipped his jacket as he spoke. "We're out of the wind—no need for so many clothes." Reaching over, he unzipped her jacket. "And, if these new sleeping bags live up to their promise, there's no need for *any* clothes. Last one undressed has to make breakfast." He flung his jacket aside and pulled off his sweatshirt.

"Wait!" she cried. "No fair. By my rules you have to turn off the lantern first."

"Why?"

"We do it my way, Mr. Confident, or I stay dressed," she announced imperiously.

He shrugged as he clicked off the lantern. "Ms. Modesty wins the round."

It wasn't really modesty, though she wasn't about to say so. Actually, she didn't want him to see her scars. Though she'd admitted she'd been injured in an accident, she'd kept her scars hidden. Once he saw where those scars were, he might guess the truth, a truth she longed to keep hidden from him forever.

CHAPTER ELEVEN

"**I** won!" Fenn announced in the darkness of the tent.

"Oh, no, you didn't," Neita countered. "It was a dead heat."

"Let me make sure," he said, his hands finding her shoulders, then easing down over her bare breasts and pausing to caress her nipples. "So far, so good." His hands dropped lower, sliding over her hips. "You're right—no clothes. But how do I know we tied?"

"Because I say so."

The betraying huskiness in her voice made Fenn smile with anticipation. She was as eager as he was. Tonight there'd be no last-minute changes of mind, no interruptions. He'd fought to keep her from going with him on this trip, but he'd lost. She was here, and they were alone together in a place that could hardly be more private. He told himself he'd go slow, he'd make the pleasure last for both of them. The future didn't exist, only tonight did—a never-ending night of love.

As he eased her down onto the yielding softness of the sleeping bags, he thought that she was where she belonged—in his arms. And he just might never let her go.

With his eyes adjusted to the dark, he noticed a faint light from the waxing moon coming through the tent fabric, though not enough to really see by. Another time he'd persuade Neita to make love in the light so he could enjoy looking at her beautiful body.

Ignoring the dark whisper in his mind, reminding him he was a Volan, he promised himself firmly that, damn it, there *would* be another time.

Then her lips met his and he ceased to think coherently. Everything about her aroused him—her smooth skin, the softness of her breasts pressed against his chest, the enticingly rounded curve of her hip, her spicy scent.

His tongue invaded her mouth, tasting her sweetness, teasing, urging, caressing. Her tiny moans of pleasure thrilled through him. When his mouth found her breasts, she arched against him, repeating his name in a sigh as her fingers threaded through his hair.

"I've wanted you from the moment I first touched you," he murmured against her mouth.

"Yes," she whispered. "Oh, yes." She longed to say more, to tell him it was more than wanting for her, but she was too bemused to try to find the words.

His kiss deepened, sending urgent messages of need throbbing through her. His caressing fingers slipped between her thighs and, caught up in passion wilder than anything she'd ever dreamed of, she reached for him.

He gasped when her hand closed around him. Easing her hand away, he pulled away for a moment that seemed to her to take forever. Then he rolled her onto her back, rose over her and eased inside.

As they joined together, she was rocked by the most incredible sensation she'd ever experienced. What she felt was more than exquisite lovemaking, more than rapturous fulfillment. She was too caught up in the fevered intensity of their union to make any attempt to understand what was happening—all she knew was that they were truly one, in every sense.

Afterward, as they lay close to one another, neither spoke for a time.

"Did you feel—?" Fenn began, then paused. "I don't even know how the hell to ask you," he went on, "because I haven't a clue as to what it was that hit me."

"Whatever it was happened to me, too," she told him.

"I thought so. Because I felt your pleasure along with mine."

"And I felt yours. As though we were together in all ways."

"Linked," he agreed. "Mind and body. I wouldn't have believed it possible." He touched her cheek. "It *isn't* possible."

"Maybe not. But it happened."

"I meant to go slow," he said, "but once you touched me I couldn't wait."

Because she could think now, she realized why he'd drawn back for that impossibly long moment. She put her fingers to his lips. "I don't have any STDs," she said. "Unless you do, there was no need to use protection."

"If you mean, can I transmit some horrible disease sexually, the answer is no. The docs assure me there's nothing wrong in that area. Just in my head."

Hearing the bitterness in his voice, she cuddled his head against her breasts.

"Mmm," he murmured, nuzzling her. "This might not cure me, but it sure takes my mind off caring whether or not I ever remember."

A high wavering cry from somewhere outside the tent made Neita pull away and sit bolt upright. "What's that?"

Before he could answer, another animal howled, its cry fainter, seemingly coming from farther away.

"Coyotes talking to each other," he said.

Realizing he'd sat up, too, she clutched his arm. "Are you sure?"

"Positive. Listen carefully to the cries."

Uneasy, but wanting to believe him, she strained her ears, hearing yet a third animal's high-pitched howl, then a cacophony of many cries mixed together.

"It almost sounds like they're arguing," she said, beginning to be convinced Fenn was right. The sounds she heard were definitely different from the howling that haunted Halfmoon House.

"Or maybe laughing," Fenn said. "Many of the native California tribes believed their creator was Coyote and that at night he laughed at the havoc he'd let loose on the earth when he made man out of adobe."

He drew her gently back down onto the sleeping bags and into his arms. "Those coyotes aren't nearby," he murmured. "And, anyway, they mean us no harm."

She snuggled against him, knowing he was right. As she relished the warm feel of his bare skin against hers, desire stirred deep inside her. She couldn't be this close to Fenn and not want to make love with him. Yet hearing the coyotes' song to the moon had leached some of the joy from their night together.

Though they might set aside all worry for the moment, forgetting everything but one another, she'd been reminded that danger lay ahead and the warning stuck like a burr in the back of her mind.

This was their night, Fenn told himself. His and Neita's. No coyote, nor anything else, was going to rob them of their chance to be together. Whatever he might become when the moon was full, he was himself tonight—he was a man. A man who held in his arms the most unusual as well as the most desirable woman in the world.

The woman he loved.

But if he truly loved her, wouldn't he find a way to make her leave him? Because how else could he keep her safe?

That's tomorrow's worry, he thought, setting it aside as desire throbbed through him. Tonight she's mine.

Sweet and arousing as caressing her was, exciting as he found her welcoming warmth, these wonders were enhanced, magnified beyond anything he'd ever imagined, once they joined together. Making love with Neita was so much more than a series of physical sensations that it was indescribable.

In some strange fashion he became Neita without losing his sense of self. The union was glorious, dizzying, mind-blowing—and he wished it would never end.

When at last they parted, he zipped the sleeping bags shut against the chill of the night air and then held her close.

"Fenn," she murmured drowsily, saying his name like a caress. "Oh, Fenn..."

He closed his eyes, happily aware that she felt the same way he did, but could find no words to describe that wondrous feeling.

Dawn came too soon. A bird perched on the tent pole and began twittering as the sun rose, a cheerful, natural sound, but as sleep-destroying as any alarm clock.

The night was over; tomorrow had arrived. Fenn, apprehensive about possible unpleasant surprises ahead, didn't welcome the new day. He glanced at Neita and found her looking at him. Her gaze warmed him, partly banishing his gloom.

"I suppose making breakfast is a joint affair," she said.

He smiled, reminded of their clothes-discarding contest. "What else?"

"Who gets up first and starts the fire?"

"When was the last time you started a campfire?" he asked.

"Would you believe never?"

He raised his eyebrows. "I'd say your education has been sadly deficient."

"I'll accept that as long as you don't tell me this morning is a fine time for me to learn."

He drew her closer and kissed her. "We could forget the fire. And breakfast."

"For a while," she whispered against his lips.

"Are all nurses so practical?" he grumbled, easing away and fumbling for the sleeping-bag zipper. She'd said aloud what he already knew. Whether he wanted to or not, it was time to get on with what he'd come to the mountains to do.

She didn't answer, watching him crawl out of the bag into the morning chill and grab up his clothes. "Counting my goose bumps?" he asked.

"No," she admitted. "Admiring what I didn't get to see last night."

He grinned his pleasure. "When do I get a turn?"

"Not this morning. Because I'm sure your good deed for the day is going to be tossing me my clothes so I can at least get partially dressed before emerging into this ice-cold dawn."

He obliged, leaving her struggling to dress inside the sleeping bag as he left the tent.

Her good humor raised his spirits, keeping his fears at bay during breakfast and on their hike up the long slope toward the cliff. But the closer they came to his destination, the more disturbed he became.

"I don't recognize anything," he said. "Theo trained me young to notice landmarks, and I do it as a matter of habit. If I'd come this way before, I ought to be able to pick out one or two familiar sights." He pointed to two toppled trees, now needleless with decay, that had fallen one over the other to form a perfect cross. "Something like that, for example."

"Wait. We're not there yet."

"You're always telling me to wait. I'm tired of waiting. I want to remember. I *need* to remember." For her sake as well as his. Didn't she understand?

"What made these gouges on this pine trunk?" she asked after they'd walked in silence for a time.

He paused to look at the tree and the deep parallel grooves, some higher than his head, that marred its bark. "A bear is my guess. He stands on his hind legs and sharpens his front claws that way."

Her eyes widened. "Like a cat, you mean?"

"I think the bear has other reasons—such as marking the boundaries of his home turf. In their way, animals can be as territorial as humans."

"Could it have been an angry bear that forced you over the cliff?"

Fenn shrugged. In his nightmare visions, something monstrous threatened him, but whatever it was remained out of focus.

The trees thinned, ending abruptly when the ground underfoot gave way to solid rock. Fenn stopped and stared at the rocky outcropping extending hundreds of feet from side to side and ten feet ahead before ending in thin air.

The rock varied in color from tan to brown. Small plants struggled to grow in its crevices. He glanced up at the sky, where wispy clouds straggled across the morning blue. To the north an eagle or a very large hawk—it was too far away to be sure—spiraled up and up.

He could swear he'd never stood in this spot before. Taking a deep breath, he walked slowly toward the brink of the cliff. Neita had hung back, almost making him forget she was along, but now she appeared at his side.

"Making certain I don't fall off again?" he asked.

"I'm curious to see how far you fell the first time," she said coolly.

They reached the edge, halting a few steps back from the very brink. Neita looked down and drew in her breath. "Oh my God!" she whispered.

Fenn forced himself to stare downward. He'd been told it was a forty-foot drop, but from here it seemed farther. The cliff face wasn't sheer; several rock shelves jutted out here and there. The ranger had told Theo that Fenn must have come to rest on one of those shelves at first and then shifted position and fell the remaining distance, making it two shorter drops rather than one long fall.

"Probably what saved his life" had been the ranger's opinion.

Fenn was about to congratulate himself on his calmness when Neita grasped his arm and pulled him backward. Only then did he realize he was trembling so hard he could barely stay on his feet.

"Sit down," she ordered when they were well back from the brink.

He didn't argue.

She sat on the rock beside him. "Were you ever troubled by a fear of heights before your amnesia?" she asked.

"I don't think so. Theo says not to his knowledge."

"Then I'd say your body was remembering that fall, even if your mind refuses to."

Fenn thought about what she'd said as he waited for his involuntary shivering to ease. He'd had no sensation of fear while looking over the cliff edge, and yet he'd certainly been affected physically. Neita could be right.

"Unfortunately," he said after a time, "I still don't have a clue as to why I fell from the cliff. Nothing in these surroundings seems familiar to me, nothing triggers any memory whatsoever."

"Are you willing to try an experiment?" she asked.

"What do you have in mind?"

"When I tell you to, I'd like you to stand up, close your eyes, and then, eyes still closed, turn around and face the woods. I'll stand to one side so I'm not in your line of vision. Do you know the rudiments of meditation?"

"I have a pretty good idea," he said.

"Do your best to blank your mind while you're facing the woods with your eyes shut. When I think you've succeeded, I'll whisper words in your ear. Open your eyes immediately and repeat those words loud and clear, say them as though you meant every word. Got it?"

Mystified but willing, he nodded.

"Okay, begin," she ordered.

Fenn rose, shut his eyes and turned in a half circle, pleased to find he was steady on his feet again. He began the breathing exercises he'd learned from a yoga instructor, persisting with them, on and on and on.

When he heard the whispering, it was as though it came from inside his head rather than into his ear from the outside. The words seemed strangely familiar.

"No!" he cried, repeating the words as he opened his eyes. "Don't come any closer!"

For a heart-stopping instant he imagined he saw a giant wolflike beast at the edge of the woods, a beast he knew was stalking him with deadly intent. Involuntarily, he took a step backward. Then another and another. And another.

"Fenn!" Neita exclaimed. "Stop!"

He blinked in bewilderment and halted. Neita—here? Why was it light not dark, day not night? There was no beast crouching to spring out of the trees at him, no beast at all. . . .

"Look at me," Neita ordered.

He glanced to his right, toward the sound of her voice. Neita stood several feet away, her eyes dark with apprehension.

"Do you know me?" Her voice quavered.

He let his breath out in a gusty sigh and nodded.

When she clasped his hand in hers and urged him forward, he looked over his shoulder and was shocked to see how close he stood to the edge of the cliff. Neita led him to the verge of the trees before she stopped.

"This time I'm the one who's shaking," she said. "I have to sit down."

When they sat side by side on the sun-warmed rock, she laid her head on his shoulder and he put his arm around her. He kept turning to eye the gloom under the trees uneasily as he tried to figure out exactly what had happened.

"What did you see when you opened your eyes and repeated my words?" she asked, easing away to gaze at him.

"I thought I saw a beast right about here. Coming at me."

"What you saw came from your memory," she told him. "I was looking at the woods, and I assure you there was no beast. You nearly gave me heart failure when you began backing toward the cliff edge. I was afraid to grab you for fear you might think you were being attacked."

"Are you saying that beast is a part of my lost memory?" Even as he asked the question, he knew the answer. In a way, even though he couldn't remember, he'd been convinced all along that something had driven him over the cliff.

"The night I arrived at Halfmoon House," she said, "you had a nightmare and woke me because you were thrashing around in your bed. When I entered your room, you were mumbling the words I whispered in your ear a few minutes ago. I thought maybe if you repeated those same words in the same place where you first said them, it was possible you'd remember what had happened." She grimaced. "My idea worked almost too well."

"The beast seemed so real, so—" He hesitated and didn't go on.

"What kind of an animal was it?"

"No ordinary animal looks like what I saw—huge, wolflike and yet not a wolf, eyes glowing in the moonlight, vicious, bloody fangs—" He broke off again and shuddered.

"Did it howl?"

"Yes. I mean, no. I didn't hear my imaginary beast howl."

"But you said yes. Why?"

"Because I know, without being aware how and why I know, that it can and does howl."

"The beast that killed Zorn," she said. "There can't be more than one."

"Werewolf," he muttered.

She glanced at him but said nothing.

Werewolf. Up until now Neita had denied the possibility of such creatures existing. Was she wrong?

Unconsciously her hand drifted to her right hip, her fingers touching the sheathed knife through the cloth of her riding pants as her grandmother's rhyme circled in her head.

> *A silver dagger keeps away*
> *What steel and iron cannot slay.*

Did the words refer to werewolves?

Reminded that Theo had seemed pleased the dagger blade was silver, she wondered if he, like Fenn, believed there were beings who could change their shapes, humans who could shift into beast forms. Surely that couldn't be possible. But *something* roamed the night, howling under the moon, a beast that had killed Zorn and apparently had also menaced Fenn in these mountains.

"Didn't you tell me werewolves shift shape only when the moon is full?" she asked.

"Or maybe a day or two before or after." He didn't seem surprised by her question. "I had my accident on the night of a full moon."

Theo had insisted she and Fenn must be back at Halfmoon House before the night of the coming full moon. Why? Did he believe the werewolf, in human form, had trailed them into the mountains? That seemed unlikely, but then so did everything else.

She'd been looking forward to spending another wonderful night in the tent with Fenn, but now fear coiled around her like a poisonous snake. True, the moon wasn't quite full, but it would be in only a few days. What protection could a tent offer?

"Let's start back to your uncle's house immediately," she blurted.

Fenn stared at her. "You're frightened."

Neita couldn't deny it. She'd been willing enough to accept what she thought of as harmless but helpful bits and pieces of her Finnish grandmother's teachings. At the same time she'd pushed aside the rest of Grandma Metsula's esoteric lore as nothing but old country beliefs of ignorant folk, beliefs that made no sense when viewed by the light of modern knowledge.

No longer. For the first time in her life she and the man she'd come to love were threatened by something she didn't understand. She was being forced to acknowledge that what she'd labeled as unbelievable might very well be true.

While her grandmother might have known how to combat a werewolf, she did not. And she was terrified.

CHAPTER TWELVE

Fenn and Neita reached Halfmoon House at dusk. "The tower light's on," Fenn said. "Uncle Theo's up there in his aerie, so he must be feeling all right."

"That's good." she said. "He wouldn't let me so much as take his pulse before he and Barnes turned back."

"He adjusted to his spinal injury better than any of us imagined he would, but not to his heart attack. Since his recovery he seems to want to deny there's anything wrong with his heart."

"Illness affects some people that way. It's hard to accept that a part of your body can fail you."

"Believe me, I know. I can't get over the feeling that my mind's betrayed me."

"Your uncle Theo may feel the same about his heart."

As they neared the garage, Neita saw Weslin's red sports car in one of the parking spaces. Had he come alone, she wondered, or was Lycia with him?

As if in answer, Fenn said, "I see my cousins are visiting."

"Do they always arrive as a pair?" she asked.

"At Uncle Theo's, they do."

Entering through the back door, they found Weslin waiting for them in the kitchen. "I thought that was your car I heard," he said to Fenn. "I was surprised to hear you'd gone off to revisit the scene of the crime, so to speak. But aren't you home a day early?"

Fenn nodded. "Is Uncle Theo okay?"

Weslin shrugged. "Much as usual, I'd say. He hasn't really snapped back from his heart attack. I can't think why you agreed to take him along on—"

"Did *you* ever come out a winner in an argument with Theo?" Fenn demanded.

Weslin smiled wryly. "I see your point."

Emily came bustling into the kitchen with Zier at her heels. The dog immediately trotted over to Neita.

"Zier and me were watching TV in my room," Emily said. "She must've heard you 'cause she pawed at the door till I opened it, and then we both came to see what was going on. I didn't expect you back so soon, Mr. Fenn. Shall I fix you and Neita a bite to eat?"

"No thanks, we ate on our way home," Fenn told her.

"I'll just go back to my program, then. Come along, Zier."

The Doberman ignored her, refusing to leave Neita's side.

"She'll be all right with me, Emily," Neita said.

"If you say so. But she'll have to be let out once more before she settles down for good. We've been keeping her in nights, you know. Her leash is hanging right there by the back door, but don't you go taking her for a run—that's Barnes's job."

"I'll remember," Neita promised.

"Good night to you all," Emily said as she left the kitchen.

"Is Lycia around?" Fenn asked Weslin.

"If you mean, did she come with me—yes. But I dropped her off in Eureka. It seems she found an old flame in town and he's giving a party tonight that she promised to hostess. I may drop in later. Want to join me? I'm sure you'd be welcome—Neita, too, for that matter."

"Not tonight, thanks," Fenn said.

"I'm beat," Neita put in, glad that she wouldn't have to go since Fenn wasn't. "A hot shower and bed has much more appeal than a party. But thanks."

Leaving Fenn in the kitchen with Weslin, Neita started up the back stairs with Zier trailing her. She hadn't reached the top before she heard Fenn's steps behind them. She slowed.

"A hot shower does sound inviting," he said, catching up. "If I can stay awake long enough to take one. I wish we could—" He broke off and shook his head.

Neita understood what he hadn't said and couldn't decide whether she was more disappointed or relieved at his decision to stay apart from her tonight.

Their unique linkage, marvelous as it had been, was also overwhelming, even awesome, in the original sense of the word—inspiring fear. She'd been somewhat of a loner all her life and suddenly here she was sharing part of herself with another in an intimacy unlike anything she'd ever known. Was Fenn, now that he'd had time to think things over, reluctant to share himself so fully with her again?

The sharing was involuntary, a part of their lovemaking, so to retreat from its fearful wonder meant giving up all involvement with each other. Could she do that? Or was it far too late?

"You look as confused as I feel," Fenn said, pausing as they reached the door to his room.

"I *am* confused," she admitted.

"We both could use a good night's sleep." He opened his door, then hesitated, frowning. "Why do I have this feeling I'm making a mistake by letting you sleep alone?"

She smiled one-sidedly and gestured at the dog. "Obviously I *won't* be alone. Good night, Fenn." As she started to go on to her own door, he caught her arm.

"It can't end," he said. "You realize we've passed the point of no return, don't you?" He bent and brushed his lips across hers. "Good night. For now."

The hot shower, rather than refreshing Neita, made her sleepier than ever. She sat on her bed in her nightshirt, yawning and eyeing Zier. "I'm supposed to see that you have a last outing before being shut in for the night," she told the dog.

Zier rested her head on Neita's knee, giving no indication she had any needs other than to be petted. Neita stroked her head. "I guess I can take the chance you'll wake me up if you get desperate—okay?"

Zier swung around to face the door, and a moment later someone tapped on it.

"Who is it?" Neita asked.

"Barnes."

After Neita pulled on her robe and opened the door, the dog refused to go with Barnes, whining and backing away from him.

He shrugged. "She'll need a last run," he said to Neita. "If it's all right with you, I'll come back later."

"I'll be asleep," she warned.

"It would be a shame to disturb you. If you don't mind my doing so, when I return I'll just open your door a bit and if Zier's ready, she'll come out on her own. When I bring her back, if she insists on being with you, I'll let her into your room again."

Neita glanced at her window, seeing a pale glow outside that she knew must be moonlight, and then looked at Barnes again. "Is it safe for you to take Zier for a run late at night?" she asked.

"We stay near the house, Zier and I." Though his answer wasn't direct, it was obvious he knew what she meant.

"I don't mind if you come back for her later," Neita said, not telling him she'd probably wake up, anyway. No matter how quietly he might open her door, she was a light sleeper.

Barnes didn't nod and turn away as she'd expected. Instead, he cleared his throat and glanced up and down the corridor. Lowering his voice, he said, "I was wondering if you could find a way to take a look at Mr. Theo in the morning without letting on what you're doing."

Neita blinked. "What's the matter with him?"

"He says nothing is. But I'd feel better if you told me that instead of him."

"Should we wait that long? I could dress and—"

"That won't be necessary," Barnes said hastily. "Morning's soon enough. It's for my own peace of mind, really. He'd be furious with both of us if I brought you to him now."

"If you're quite certain he's not in any danger."

"I am. You'll try to be casual about it tomorrow, won't you?"

"I'll do my best," Neita promised.

She closed the door on Barnes and climbed into bed. Zier watched her, then turned around several times and finally settled herself on the rug beside the bed.

Neita had half expected that the new worry over Theo's health, added to her own problems, might keep her awake, but almost immediately she sank like a stone into a deep well of sleep.

Later, she was partly roused by a sound she vaguely identified as her door closing. Believing it was Barnes collecting Zier, she drifted off again.

When she next roused, she came fully awake, her heart pounding in alarm. Sitting up, she reached for the bedside lamp, then held, realizing the moon cast enough light to see. No one was in her room and she heard nothing unusual. What had awakened her? Was it the dog? She swung her feet over the edge of the bed and felt for Zier with her toes. The dog wasn't on the rug.

"Zier?" she said softly.

There was no response. Perhaps Barnes had kept the dog with him. The door to the hall was closed. She padded over to check the connecting door, found it shut and frowned. She'd left it ever so slightly ajar. Easing the door open, she peered into Fenn's room. His curtains were drawn, shutting out the moonlight. She padded over to his bed. Empty. Oh, no, not again, she thought apprehensively.

She flicked on the light. Fenn was nowhere in his room or his bathroom, and the hall door stood open.

Her skin prickling with alarm, Neita dashed back into her room for her robe and slippers and was halfway through her own door when she stopped abruptly.

Never again would she leave her knife behind. Returning to her room, she eased the sheathed silver dagger from under her pillow and slid it into the pocket of her robe.

A quick search of the downstairs didn't turn up Fenn, but she hadn't really expected to find him inside. If he was sleepwalking again, most likely he'd leave the house as he'd done before. The front door, she discovered, was closed but unlocked, strengthening her belief that he'd gone out.

Taking a deep breath, she eased the door open and ventured into the moonlit night. Fenn was nowhere in sight. As she skirted the house, calling his name, she tried to imagine where he might have gone. With no way to be sure, she needed the dog. She'd have to go back inside and get Zier from wherever Barnes had left her.

Neita turned to reenter the house when she heard a faint whining coming from the direction of the kennels. Could Barnes have left Zier there? But why? And was it Zier she heard? She called the dog's name and the whining grew louder, punctuated with barks.

Zier greeted her with frenzied leaps at the wire fencing. The metal gate to the kennel was closed, but the chain and padlock were gone. When Neita opened the door, Zier almost bowled her over in her hurry to be free. But she didn't go far before returning to Neita's side.

Once she'd soothed the agitated Zier somewhat, Neita said, "Find Fenn."

Instead of circling or putting her nose to the ground to pick up scent, Zier growled, crowding against Neita, the dog's hackles raised as she stared in the direction of the gazebo.

"Is it Fenn?" Neita whispered to the dog.

Zier's only answer was to snarl, her teeth showing, still facing the same direction, shudders running through her body. Her fear communicated itself to Neita. Whatever the dog sensed couldn't possibly be Fenn. Zier was doing her best to warn that something dangerous prowled the night.

Realizing she was a fool to stand around waiting to be attacked, Neita turned and raced toward the house, one hand gripping the hilt of the silver dagger, pulled free of its sheath. At first Zier ran with her, then suddenly the dog was gone. Neita glanced over her shoulder and gasped in horror to see Zier streaking toward a dark and fearsome shape that had seemingly appeared from nowhere.

The beast! Wherever it had come from, the beast was after her, racing toward her. Neita ran as fast as she could, in her terror casting frequent looks behind her to see how close the beast was. She saw Zier launch herself at the beast, heard the dog's anguished howl as the monster flung Zier aside and kept on racing toward her, closer and closer.

With the front door in sight, Neita tripped over an unseen obstruction and, unable to catch herself, sprawled forward onto the grass. Knowing she'd never be able to regain her feet before the beast attacked, in desperation she flung herself over onto her back and raised the tiny dagger.

"Silver!" she screamed as the horror loomed over her, jaws slavering, fangs gleaming in the moonlight. "It's silver!"

She jabbed at the beast with the knife, felt the blade sink in. For a long moment time seemed suspended, and then a heavy weight thudded down on top of Neita, covering her chest and face and cutting off her breath. Everything faded into darkness.

Neita drifted, cut loose from the world, belonging nowhere, a piece of flotsam. Only one tiny thread connected her anywhere, one small thread prevented her from floating away. And someone tugged on that thread, urging her back from the dark void.

"Neita," he called. "Neita!" She could hear pain in his voice—pain and fear. "Oh, God, what have I done?" he cried.

His voice was familiar but she couldn't understand what was troubling him. Another sound intermixed with his voice—an animal whimpering. A dog.

Zier. And then Neita understood she'd been pulled all the way back to Halfmoon House, and she realized who the man was. Her eyes fluttered open and she stared into Fenn's anguished face.

Other voices came from nearby, asking what was wrong, asking what had happened. Weslin. Barnes.

Fenn gathered her into his arms. She clung to him as he rose with her. "Zier," she murmured weakly. "She's hurt."

"I'll take care of Zier," Barnes said.

"What the hell happened?" Weslin demanded, walking beside them as Fenn carried her toward the open front door.

"Something attacked me," she whispered.

"I found Neita lying on the lawn with Zier draped over her," Fenn said. "The dog was slashed and bleeding, evidently from trying to protect her. I think—I hope—most of the blood is Zier's."

Only then did Neita realize she was covered with blood. Yet as far as she could tell, she didn't think she'd been badly injured.

"Do you know what attacked you?" Weslin asked her.

"The beast," she whispered, the words sticking in her throat. Reaction to the frightening attack, as well as the smell and the unpleasant stickiness of blood, made her dizzy. She rested her cheek against Fenn's bare chest, realizing belatedly that his chest was blood-smeared.

Bile rose in her throat and she swallowed repeatedly, dimly aware they'd entered the house and that Fenn was carrying her upstairs.

"Shall I send Emily up?" Weslin asked from below, in the entry.

"No!" Fenn snapped. "I'll take care of Neita myself."

Take care of has two different meanings, she thought hazily. But of course she had nothing to fear from Fenn.

"How do you feel?" he asked when they reached his room. "Can you stand up?"

"I think so."

Without another word, he pushed through the open door, carried her into the bathroom, turned on the shower and stepped inside with her. He eased her onto her feet and, as the warm water sluiced over them both, stripped off her sodden robe and sleepshirt, as well as the bottoms of his pajamas, all he was wearing.

By the time he shut off the water and helped her from the shower, Neita was feeling more like herself. Once the blood had been washed away, she realized none of it was, in fact, hers. She wasn't injured. She took the towel from him when he started to dry her, saying, "I can do that myself."

As she used the towel, she glanced at Fenn and drew in her breath. He *had* been hurt. Blood oozed from a small gash on his left chest. Her first thought was to tend to him, so she hastily wrapped the damp towel around her.

"Let me take a look at that wound," she said.

He glanced down at himself, seeming surprised to find his chest bleeding.

"Zier snapped at me when I moved her off you," he said after a moment. "She must have connected."

The gash was fairly deep, like something a dog's fang might make. She cleaned it again with soap and water and taped on several sterile gauze pads she found in his medicine cabinet.

"Have you had a tetanus booster recently?" she asked.

He nodded. "After my accident. That's enough fussing over me—let's get you to bed."

"I can manage on my own," she assured him.

"No way am I going to let you out of my sight until morning." He marched her through the connecting door.

In her bedroom, her back to him, she removed the towel and donned a clean nightgown. By the time she turned around, he was reaching for her hand. "Back to my room. You get the bed, I'll take the couch. No arguments."

"I'm worried about Zier," she said once he'd tucked her into his bed as though he was the nurse and she the patient.

"Barnes knows how to treat her injuries. He's good with animals."

"She saved my life. I saw her attack the beast and fail. Then she must have tried to protect me by covering me with her body." Her voice faltered on the last few words as she relived those terrible moments.

Fenn, who'd been leaning over her, straightened and turned away. "Zier's very attached to you."

"Did you see—" she began.

"I heard Zier scream in pain and I came running," he interrupted. "I didn't see the beast."

Neita bit her lip, wondering why he'd turned his back. "You were already outside," she said. "Sleepwalking."

He strode to the couch and slumped down on it, staring into the cold hearth. "I thought I was over that sleepwalking business, but I was wrong. I blame myself for your attack. You came to look for me, otherwise you'd have been safe in bed. I don't know why the hell I was wandering around the grounds. Zier's cry brought me to myself, and I knew something terrible had happened."

"Don't blame yourself for something you can't control," she said.

"I thought you were dead." His voice was rough. "And the worst of it is—" He broke off and buried his face in his hands.

Neita slid from the bed, padded to the couch and sat beside him, her hand stroking his shoulders. "I found

Zier in the kennels," she said after a time. "I wonder why she was there."

Fenn raised his head. "For all I know, *I* could have put her in the kennels."

Since it might be true, she didn't comment. "Thinking back," she said, "I realize the beast never did howl. It seemed to materialize out of thin air with no warning at all."

He turned to her and gathered her into his arms. "I don't want to lose you." Making no attempt to kiss her, he held her close to him.

She sighed, relaxing in his embrace, wanting no more than the warmth and comfort of his arms. Here, with Fenn, she was safe. He eased her down until they lay side by side on the couch, then he pulled the afghan over them. The terror of the night faded from her mind, the danger was past and they were together.

She was almost asleep when she remembered her knife. "My silver dagger," she said, stirring. "Did you happen to find it?"

"Picked the knife off the ground and put it in the pocket of your robe," he murmured drowsily.

She settled back, relieved she hadn't lost the knife, as she might very well have because she'd stabbed at the beast when it loomed over her. Neita grimaced as she remembered the feel when the point of the dagger sunk into the beast's chest.

The beast's chest?

Against her will, she visualized the small, penetrating wound she'd just cleaned and bandaged. On Fenn's chest.

A coincidence, that's all it was. She refused to believe anything else. Maybe such monstrosities as werewolves could exist, but Fenn couldn't possibly be one. Never!

Yet the words he'd said as he bent over her bloodied body returned to haunt her: *Oh, God, what have I done?*

CHAPTER THIRTEEN

Near dawn, Neita extricated herself from Fenn's relaxed embrace and, leaving him sleeping on the couch, returned to her room. Feeling exhausted—her rest had been fitful and plagued by dark dreams—she climbed into her own bed.

She woke to a gray morning with rain beading her window and someone tapping at her door. Glancing at the clock, she was shocked to find it was nearly eleven. She jumped from the bed and crossed the room to find Barnes in the corridor with Zier. The dog immediately pushed through the partly open door into the room.

"Sorry to disturb you," Barnes said, "but I couldn't keep Zier content any longer—she was determined to be with you."

Neita crouched to hug the dog, being careful to avoid the gashes along Zier's side.

"All that blood made her injuries look worse than they were," Barnes said. "After I cleaned her up, I found the cuts weren't deep and should heal without stitches, so I didn't take her to the vet. She hates going there."

"Zier would have died for me," Neita murmured, tears welling in her eyes.

"I believe you're right," Barnes said. "If you don't mind, I'll leave her here."

"Yes, please do." Neita blinked away the tears, rose and, once Barnes had left, began dressing. She chose a bright yellow shirt and a gold skirt to counteract the gloomy day as well as her dismal spirits. Zier watched her every move.

"I overslept," Neita told her. "Private-duty nurses aren't supposed to do that."

Zier's gaze was all-forgiving—obviously she didn't mind.

Neita sighed. Since arriving at Halfmoon House she'd managed to overstep the parameters of her nursing duties in about every way she could. Perhaps it was time she left. Or possibly past time.

Before she came to any decision, though, she had to fulfill her promise to Barnes to evaluate Theo's health. And, whether she wanted to face the problem or not, there was Fenn to consider.

Taking a look at Theo would be the easiest.

She tapped on the connecting door before leaving her room. When there was no answer, she opened it and peered in. Fenn wasn't in the room, but that was no surprise, it being so late. She went downstairs with the dog at her heels.

"Mr. Fenn's in the library playing chess with Mr. Weslin," Barnes told her when she asked him. He cleared his throat. "Mr. Theo would like to talk to you. He asked me to bring you to the tower room at your convenience—perhaps after you've eaten, if that suits you?"

"Has he been told what happened last night?" she asked, thinking that was why Theo was asking for her.

"Mr. Fenn spoke to him, yes."

"I really don't need to eat before—" she began.

Barnes interrupted. "Mr. Theo would never forgive me if I rushed you up to the tower without allowing you time for breakfast."

"All right then—fifteen minutes?"

Barnes nodded and left her. Neita went on to the kitchen where Emily was mixing salad greens for lunch.

"I'll just have a quick cup of coffee right here in the kitchen," she told Emily.

Emily shot her a reproving look. "Coffee's not enough. You need something to go along with it. I made my special cinnamon rolls for breakfast—it'll take less than a minute to heat up a few in the microwave." She glanced at Zier, who'd settled down at Neita's feet. "And I'll find a snack for the dog, too."

Neita didn't try to argue, aware Emily would be insulted if she turned down the offer of rolls.

"These smell heavenly," Neita told her, when Emily set the warmed rolls on the kitchen table. "I love the cinnamon scent."

"They taste as good as they smell, if I do say so myself," Emily told her. "Ms. Lycia, now, she never listens to me—lives on coffee, she does. Had her brother bring a carafe to her room a bit ago. Says she's under the weather. Huh! Too much partying last night, if you ask me. Heaven only knows when she dragged in, but at least she missed all that hullabaloo we had around here."

Emily shook her head. "Such awful goings-on. I told Mr. Theo straight out that something's got to be done about that monster. He promised me—very solemn he was, too—that he'd see to it."

What did Theo intend to do? Neita wondered. Hire armed guards? But would ordinary bullets bring down this particular beast?

"It's a wonder how that dog has taken to you," Emily went on as she set a dish containing slices of roast chicken on the floor for Zier. "She's going to be heartbroken when you leave."

Neita sighed. Zier wouldn't be the only one heartbroken. Difficult as it would be to leave the dog she'd grown so fond of, parting from Fenn would be a million times worse. And yet how could she remain here? It wasn't so much the danger as her own unnerving suspicion that she wanted to flee from....

Though her appetite had vanished, she forced herself to finish a second roll and another cup of coffee before rising from the table. "Delicious, Emily," she said. "They *do* taste as good as they smell."

Barnes was hovering in the entry, obviously waiting for her. "Mr. Theo won't mind if Zier comes up with you," he said. "I'm sure he'd prefer not to have her down here whining the entire time you were gone."

The small elevator off the entry was barely large enough to hold her, Barnes and the dog. When it stopped and the doors opened, Neita found they were actually in the tower's one large room. Barnes stepped out first.

"I've brought Ms. Metsula and Zier," he told Theo, who was sitting in his wheelchair facing the elevator.

"Thank you, Barnes," Theo said. Neita noticed he was was once again wearing his black gloves.

Barnes nodded and stepped back into the elevator. When its doors had closed, Theo asked, "What do you think of my lair?"

With glass panels enclosing half the room, she thought the view on a clear day must be spectacular. Even the rain spatters didn't completely hide the vista. "I can see why you spend so much time in the tower," she said, glancing around. "Fenn calls it your aerie."

The sides of the room not taken up by the elevator or the full-length windows were lined with book-packed shelves. A deep-toned red oriental rug covered the wood floor and the room was lit by unobtrusive ceiling lights. The only furniture was a round table, a small chest of drawers and a comfortable-looking recliner.

"Perching up here is certainly preferable to denning underground," he said. "Better an eagle's aerie than living like a mole. Since my accident on the basement stairs, I no longer use the vault at all. Not that I could get to it even if I wanted to."

"I believe Fenn mentioned a locked underground vault that he and his cousins only saw the inside of once."

"I've always valued my privacy. But I find that now the tower suits my purposes. Interesting, isn't it, how calamity sometimes proves to be a blessing in disguise?"

Did he really view as a blessing the fall down the basement steps that had left him paralyzed below the waist? It was hard to believe.

"I sometimes nap up here in the recliner," Theo said, abruptly changing the subject. "It's really quite comfortable. Do sit down."

Neita had been edging closer to Theo as she tried to decide if his face looked grayer than usual or whether it was the dreariness of the day. Feeling she had to obey, she crossed to the recliner, telling herself that before she left she'd bring the conversation around to how he felt. Zier, who'd stuck like a burr to Neita's side, followed her. Once she sat in the recliner, the dog leaned against the chair, resting her head on Neita's knee, her gaze fixed on Theo.

"Wounded in action saving you, I understand," Theo said, his gesture indicating the dog. "I'm sorry you were subjected to such a frightening ordeal. I hope you won't find it too hard on your nerves to repeat your version of what happened last night. Why, for instance, did you leave the house?"

Taking a deep breath, Neita let the air out slowly and began her account. Though she did her best not to relive the terror of the night as she spoke of it, by the time she was close to finishing she was hugging herself against an inner chill.

"When I came to, Fenn was bending over me," she said. "It wasn't until later that I discovered it hadn't been the beast who fell on top of me, but Zier, trying to protect me."

Theo remained silent for a time. "You say you wounded the beast with your silver dagger?" he asked finally.

"I'm sure I did—although I don't think I could have hurt the beast much."

"You forget the blade is silver."

"I didn't forget," Neita said. "In fact, I recall screaming, 'It's silver!' at the beast, as if that would make it turn tail." Now or never, she told herself. *He* brought up the silver dagger, and this time I don't intend to let him drop the subject.

Unclasping her arms, she leaned forward. "Before you left us in the mountains, you suggested that my silver dagger was my protection but you didn't tell me against what. Do you believe, as Fenn seems to, that silver is poisonous to—werewolves?" It took some effort to push the last word out, but she managed.

"I *know* silver poisons them. And can kill them."

She stared at him, taken aback. Whatever she'd expected him to say, this wasn't it.

Theo waved a hand at the shelves of books. "My esoteric reference library. Half the volumes there have to do with shapeshifters, including werewolves. Many of the books are in other languages and some are manuscripts so ancient they're handwritten. Werewolf lore comes from all areas of the world where wolves exist or once existed.

"There's a word for werewolf in the language of every one of those countries—the Greeks called them *vrykolakas,* the Romans *versipellis,* the Norse countries *vargulfr,* the French *loup-garou,* the Spanish *lobombre,* and so on. As for the Celts—the good St. Patrick didn't just rid Ireland of snakes but also turned the Welsh king, Vereticus, into a wolf for his sins.

"Today we're so scientifically oriented, so modern in thought that no one believes in werewolves. You, for example, are still trying to deny there can possibly be such a creature as a shapeshifter."

"I—I don't want to believe in them."

"Even after you've been attacked by one?"

Neita shook her head. "You can't know for sure."

Theo wheeled his chair closer to the recliner, making Zier shift uneasily. "I can and I do. Look at me, Neita. Look closely. Do you see a crazy old man?"

She searched his face and was disturbed to note his pallor. Wasn't there also a bluish tinge to his lips? Alarmed, all thoughts of werewolves fled her mind.

"I see a very sick man," she blurted. "Not in mind, but in body." As she leaned over to reach for his wrist, Zier half whined, half growled, but Neita ignored the dog. Finding Theo's pulse thready and irregular, she rose from the chair. "Do you have your medication with you?"

"I'm wearing a nitro patch—for what help that is."

"You need to call your doctor immediately."

"No." Theo's refusal was emphatic. "What I need I already have on hand. You. You have the power to keep me going through the full moon and you must use that power. Don't argue—we both know you're a healer, among other things, and that you *can* help me."

"But you need more," she protested. "Anything I can do would only be temporary. In the hospital you'd have all the—"

"I'm not going to any hospital. If I leave Halfmoon House before the moon begins to wane, Fenn is doomed. That's the plain and simple truth, and I think in your heart of hearts you know it's true."

The truth. His words pierced painfully through Neita. Was Theo confirming her suspicions? Was Fenn really a—? No, she couldn't, she wouldn't even think the word!

"We both love Fenn," Theo said. "We both want him to survive, and to do that he needs both of us alive and here at Halfmoon House during this full moon. Therefore, you have to discard any notion of doctors or hospitals for me. Instead, you must help me yourself. Lend me some of your special power, Neita. For Fenn."

She bit her lip. "With all my heart and soul I want to help Fenn, but to do so at your expense—" She broke off. "Why is this full moon so critical? The beast is outside. If we all remain in the house, we'll be safe."

"Stop trying to reject what I've explained to you— there isn't time for such foolishness. Can't you understand? At night, when the moon is full, inside is no safer than outside, locked doors make no difference. Neither does garlic, hemlock, solanum, crucifixes or any other so-called charms against shapeshifters. Think about it, Neita. If a werewolf is human at all times except when the moon is full, how can anyone identify him? How can you be sure he isn't already inside the house in his human form?"

Apprehension shuddered through her. He *did* believe Fenn could change shape!

"Don't any of those books suggest ways to recognize a werewolf who looks like a human?" she asked.

"You still miss the point. Shapeshifters *are* human. With, of course, a genetic flaw. A curse, you might call it. But most of—" He hesitated, then, rubbing his gloved hands together, continued, "Most of them look absolutely human. Unless the moon is full."

"Can no one tell the difference? What about animals? Wouldn't they—"

"Animals fear the beast a shapechanger becomes, but not the human he is most of the time. The one exception doesn't happen to be relevant to this situation. No more talk. We can't afford to waste time that I don't have. Please take Zier down to Barnes and tell him to keep the dog shut in one room—yours, perhaps—until you're free. While you're doing that, I'll descend to my bedroom. Come to me there as soon as possible."

Further argument, she saw, wouldn't sway Theo from his resolve. Since she couldn't force him to accept medical help against his will, she nodded reluctantly, agreeing to follow his direction.

He didn't get into the elevator with her and Zier—the wheelchair would have made it very close quarters and the dog was definitely skittish about being near Theo. She'd been an outdoor dog until very recently—probably she wasn't used to the wheelchair.

After Neita handed over Zier to Barnes, she hurried to Theo's darkened bedroom. He'd transferred himself from the wheelchair to a hospital-type bed that could be elevated for comfort. Dark curtains shut out what daylight there was.

"I'd prefer no lamp be lit," he said. "Please sit beside me on the bed."

She did as he asked.

"You must decide here and now whether you can trust me," he told her. "I'll try to be as honest as I can with you, and I hope you'll extend me the same courtesy. What I see when I look at you is an aura of power surrounding you. Are you able to identify individuals who have power?"

"I've never thought of it as power," she said slowly, "but I do sense light or darkness within people. I think of them as sunshine or shadow people or neither, and I've learned to avoid the shadow people."

"What do you sense about *me?*"

She hesitated, choosing her words with care. "Part of the reason I accepted your offer to come to Halfmoon House is because I'm drawn to sunshine people and I could feel your inner glow. You asked me to be honest, so I must add that at times I've sensed your glow fading and growing dark."

"And Fenn?"

"I've never felt any shadow within Fenn, despite—" She broke off. "What I mean is, I wouldn't have remained here if I'd discovered Fenn was one of the shadow people." And I certainly wouldn't have fallen in love with him, she added to herself.

"Weslin? Lycia? Barnes? Emily?"

"They're like most people I meet. Neither sunshine nor shadow."

"Why do you think my glow is fading?" Theo asked.

"You're very ill."

"Have you noted illness diminishing the glow in others? Does illness create shadows?"

Patrick's youthful face, distorted by crazed determination, flashed before her. Because she'd dismissed the growing shadow she'd sensed within Patrick, he was dead and she was . . . maimed.

"I've learned that mental disorder can bring shadows," she said, the words bitter on her tongue.

"Let me assure you, then, that I'm not losing my mind," Theo said. "Nor am I an evil person. I have never wished to harm anyone. But, yes, I know the shadow you sense within me. That shadow has been with me most of my life. Because I have power, I've been able to fight against succumbing. As I promised, I've been as honest as I can. Will you still lend me your power?''

Remembering what had happened with Patrick, she didn't answer immediately, fearing what might happen if she agreed to what Theo asked. And yet, she did believe he wanted desperately to help Fenn. So desperately he was willing to risk his life. Shouldn't she be willing to take some risk herself?

''If I can help you, I will,'' she told Theo. ''I've never tried to heal anyone who understood exactly what I was doing. Ordinarily I use the laying on of hands.''

''We've already shared power,'' he said. ''When we held hands in the mountains. For us, that's the best way.''

''I'm willing to try. But I think it might work better if we both meditate for a few moments first.''

''Before we begin anything, Neita, I have a confession to make. Since we must touch skin to skin, I'll have to remove my gloves. I suffer from a periodic condition that distorts my hands, so I'm sure they won't feel normal to you.''

''As long as I know ahead of time, it shouldn't matter,'' she assured him, wondering what the periodic disease could be. Aware distraction of any kind could prevent her from easing into meditation, she deliberately cleared her mind.

After unknown minutes had passed, she reached for Theo's hands, finding them readily despite her closed eyes. Not allowing herself to notice any oddity, she grasped his hands in hers and visualized the star of power blazing over her head. Soon she felt its emanations—golden rays of healing—pour into her, through her, traveling along her arms, her hands, and from there into Theo's hands where they would, she knew, disperse throughout his body, bringing strength to his failing heart, strength he was borrowing to buy him the time he needed.

When the golden outpouring ceased, she dropped his hands with a sigh, feeling completely drained, as she always did after a successful healing. Only then did it occur to her that his palms had felt leathery and that his fingernails seemed unusually long. But the realization was vague—she didn't retain details while she was healing.

"Thank you, my dear," Theo said, his stronger voice and deeper intonation making her aware he was better, at least temporarily.

"You've not only helped me greatly," he continued, "but our contact has shown me that your power isn't limited to healing. You're far more powerful than you think. Remember, whether you understand how to use it or not, the power is there within you, waiting to be tapped. Never give way to despair."

Neita was too tired to take in the implications of what he'd said. All she could concentrate on was reaching her room and dropping onto her bed to rest.

Zier, waiting in her room, was overjoyed to see her—as if Neita had been away years instead of hours. She gave the dog a few consoling pats and then literally fell onto the bed and into a regenerating sleep.

She was dimly aware that someone opened a door and took the dog away. What finally did rouse her to complete alertness was the knowledge that someone was watching her. She raised her head to look around. Fenn stood in the open connecting door, holding Zier's collar to keep the dog at his side.

"You've been with my uncle," Fenn said, advancing into the room. He released Zier, who padded to the bed and stretched out on the carpet.

Neita pushed herself into a sitting position and propped pillows behind her. Even before she glanced at the clock, the dim light warned her it must be late afternoon.

"How is Theo?" Fenn asked, stepping over Zier to sit on the bed. "He looked like death warmed over when I talked to him this morning.

"Better," she said cautiously. "But not well. He's asked me to look after him for a few days."

Fenn frowned. "Can't you persuade him to go to the hospital?"

"I'm sure you're aware that your uncle makes his own decisions and once he's made them he's not easily swayed."

"You shouldn't stay here. Doesn't he realize that?"

"Fenn, he needs me. I can't leave him." You need me, too, she thought, feeling the tug of the bond between them. Whatever you are, you need me. How can I desert you?

He leaned toward her, bracing himself with an arm to either side of her while he stared into her eyes. "Do you know what I dream of?" he asked. "Do you know I dream of running down prey like a beast and then feasting on the bloody kill? What if I'm responsible for Jethro's disappearance, as Lycia believes? What if I killed the poor bastard and hid his body?"

For a moment or two she was paralyzed by the horrible images he conjured up, then she shook her head, refusing to be intimidated. "What if, what if. Make up your mind—do you want me to believe you killed Jethro while in a somnambulistic trance? Or would you prefer I believe you changed into a werewolf first?" For some reason, making light of her own suspicions eased her fears, at least for the moment.

He shifted position and gripped her shoulders, anger darkening his eyes. "Don't you understand you could be next?"

She fought free of him, fueled by her own anger. "I'm damned tired of you telling me I'm your next victim! Even if you did see a stupid pentagram on my palm, how do you know what the hell it means? And don't you dare mention your Aunt Hensa again. I've heard more than enough about her. So you've got strange relatives, so what? Most families have a weirdo or two tucked away in their past—I have at least one in mine."

She stabbed her forefinger hard against his breastbone. "Listen up. You are *not* going to kill me, do you hear?" She glanced at the window, noted it was still raining and added, "And certainly not tonight, because there won't be any moonlight to change by."

He blinked, his ferocious scowl vanishing. He began to chuckle, then roared with laughter. "It's not funny," he gasped. "I don't know why the hell I'm laughing."

"Because you're as fed up with living on the edge of terror as I am," she told him, her anger dissipating. "Why not laugh?"

"If I laugh," he said, "everyone laughs." With that he grabbed her, wrestled her down onto her back and began tickling her, making her sputter and giggle.

In no time at all, the playfulness altered course. His mouth found hers, releasing her latent desire as he revealed his own desire and laughter became passion.

"I could be talked into making love with you," he murmured. After a pause, he added, "Providing Zier lets us, that is."

Neita opened her eyes and found the dog had her forefeet on the bed, with her muzzle inches from their heads, watching them with such a puzzled look in her eyes that Neita began to laugh all over again.

And then Zier needed to go for a walk. They both took her, all three coming back to the house wet. By then it was time for dinner.

Theo sat at the head of the table, looking so well that Neita couldn't believe her eyes. Weslin joined them, but not Lycia.

"I'm afraid she had a bit too much to drink at that party last night," Weslin explained. "She's got the great-grandmother of all hangovers."

"A hangover," Theo repeated, his voice flat. "Overindulging in liquor is something a Volan should never do—she ought to be aware of that by now. I'll give her tonight to recover, but she's to be told that I expect to see her for breakfast in the morning. No excuses accepted."

"Is it an allergy to liquor, like the one Volans have to cats?" Neita asked. "Because if it is, maybe I ought to take a look at Lycia. She could be having an allergic reaction."

"No need," Weslin put in hastily. "She's not all that bad, she just isn't up to facing food yet."

"Or cats." Fenn said the words absently, without looking at any of them, almost as though he was unaware he'd spoken. He stared down at the ebony-handled brass flatware fork in his hand as though it held the secret of the ages.

Neita glanced at her own tableware—beautiful brass forks, knives and spoons—and shrugged, unable to fathom his line of thought. Cats and the tableware seemed to have no connection whatsoever. Theo, she noticed, was gazing intently at Fenn while Weslin totally ignored him.

She sensed dark undercurrents she couldn't comprehend. The uneasiness she'd shaken during the time she and Fenn spent together returned, stronger than ever.

Laughter didn't last long at Halfmoon House.

CHAPTER FOURTEEN

Neita woke to a bright day. The rain had stopped and sunlight glinted on the drops beading the shrubbery. In the morning room where she and Fenn ate breakfast, silence reigned. The night had been uneventful—apparently Fenn had slept through it undisturbed, as she had. She didn't know why he'd drawn into himself but she resented being shut out.

Though the somberness of his mood kept her from any attempt to make light conversation, Neita finally rebelled at sitting through the rest of the meal as mute as melba toast.

"This morning might be a good time to go down to the Reynolds's farm," she said as she poured herself a second cup of coffee. "We've never given Robbie that pup tent we bought for him at the camp store."

Fenn's glance was so forbidding that she bristled. What she'd suggested was harmless enough—why was he being so difficult? Before either of them could speak, Theo rolled into the room.

"I couldn't help overhearing," Theo said. "I'm afraid your trip to the farm would be wasted. The Reynolds are away for ten days. They've taken Robbie to Disneyland."

Fenn turned a searching gaze on his uncle. "Your suggestion?"

Theo shrugged. "I merely mentioned to Larry that October was a good month because Disneyland would be less crowded, with all the schools in session."

"Then you *were* involved."

"To a degree, yes." Theo's tone made it evident he didn't care to pursue the subject.

His color was good and his voice strong, Neita was pleased to see. She hoped he'd remain in improved health, even while she feared he wouldn't.

"To the degree of bankrolling their trip?" Fenn persisted.

"Not exactly." Theo switched from defense to attack. "This is a fine day for a walk, though. I suggest you and Neita take a ramble with Zier." Theo nodded at the dog sitting beside Neita's chair. "Zier needs the exercise, I'm sure Neita could do with an outing, as well, and I know she won't go without you."

Neita waited, aware his uncle was once again maneuvering Fenn into doing what he wanted him to. Fenn could refuse, but if he did, he'd sound like a grouch.

Fenn's nod was reluctant.

"How is Lycia this morning?" Neita asked when neither man said anything more.

"I'm on my way to her room now," Theo said.

"If you think there's anything I can do to help her, please let me know."

"I've been told there's no real cure for what's ailing her," Theo said. "A hangover, that is."

Basically, he was right, Neita thought. There were dozens of so-called cures for hangovers, but what one person swore was effective rarely helped someone else.

After Theo rolled from the room, Fenn said, "Hasn't little Ms. Fix-it learned by now that the world is full of people with problems that can't be solved and illnesses that can't be cured?"

Refusing to react to the bitterness in his tone, she said mildly, "That doesn't mean I can't try to alleviate the symptoms in one way or another. In Lycia's case, if she's truly allergic to alcohol and can't resist drinking it, she ought to try counseling."

Fenn set his coffee cup onto its saucer with a clatter, seeming about to offer a sharp retort.

When he didn't speak, Neita added, "Allergies can be treated in different ways. Lycia, for example, should avoid both cats and alcohol. Or she could—"

"From Marianne's account," Fenn interrupted, "Tiger behaved as though *he* were allergic to Lycia. Have you been secretly counseling the cat about avoidance?"

Neita finished her coffee before replying, determined not to allow Fenn to provoke her into a quarrel. "When do you want to take the walk?" she asked.

"May as well get my exercise early," he muttered.

Once they were in the open air, with Zier trotting beside Neita, Fenn's mood lightened. "Let's head for the ocean," he suggested. "I never did show you our secret trail down from the cliffs to the beach. We called it *Ni visovivatsa.*"

"That sounds like Russian. What's it mean?"

"I'll tell you when we reach the trail—the translation will make more sense."

"Are you fluent in Russian?" she asked.

"Uncle Theo hired a tutor to teach us Russian when we were kids. He said it was part of our Volan heritage. For a while we found it great fun to speak to one another at school in a language no one else understood. Lycia especially enjoyed it. She's always loved secrets."

They passed the flat-topped rock split open by a growing sapling that Neita remembered, but they didn't go near the old stone church. She caught a glimpse of the ruins from a distance and thought of the cape they'd found hanging inside. For a moment, darkness seemed to cloud the sunshiny day.

Pushing away even the memory of the cape, she said firmly, "What beautiful weather."

Fenn glanced at her. "You mean you've just noticed?"

"I was reminding myself."

As they neared the edge of the cliffs, a brisk sea breeze tousled her hair as it brought the scent of the ocean—salt? iodine? fish? Whatever the smell, she breathed it in with pleasure, smiling at Fenn when they stopped to rest.

"Have you ever thought you'd like to have lived in the days of the windjammers?" she asked. "How exciting it must have been to skim the waves in a clipper ship."

"My ancestors *were* seafaring men," he told her. "That's how the Volans made their fortune."

Gazing at him, she imagined him at the helm of the *Flying Cloud,* one of the fastest clipper ships of all time. "If you grew a beard and donned a captain's cap," she said, "you'd look perfectly at home on the deck of one of your ancestors' sailing ships."

"I have the feeling some of the Volans had good reason never to go to sea." He stared out over the ocean as he spoke. "We're named for the wolf, don't forget, and the wolf has always been an omen of disaster and doom."

Lately every conversation with Fenn sooner or later led to werewolves, so Neita decided to try to discuss them in a sane and sensible fashion. "In his tower, your uncle has shelf after shelf of books about shapeshifters," she said. "He seems fascinated by the subject."

Fenn nodded. "When I was fifteen and the twins thirteen—we were convalescing at the time—he told us a Russian fairy tale about the spirits of the forest, the *Lieshui.* These are powerful spirits who resent the encroachment of humans into their domain. If a man dares to defy them, the *Lieshui* allow him one warning before doom befalls him at their hands. Theo's story was about a village man who ignored this warning and so was changed into a ferocious werewolf."

"Then what happened?" she asked. "So far that's only half a fairy tale."

He turned to look at her. "I'm not sure you want to hear the rest. Russian stories are full of shadows, and this one is no exception."

"Tell me, anyway."

"The villagers greatly feared this man-wolf who daily threatened their lives," he said. "After no one, not even the village Wise Woman, could devise a charm to break the spell, each family brought one of their precious silver religious icons to the smith. He melted down the icons and fashioned a sharp-bladed silver sword that the Wise Woman swore would end the life of the werewolf.

"But no man could be found brave enough to enter the forest with the sword to confront the beast. Finally the young woman who'd been his intended bride took up the sword and waited until the wolf's hour—midnight—before she crept into the dark recesses of the forest. She believed that her beloved would rather be dead than be forced to live his life as a beast. She was certain she wouldn't survive the encounter, but she told herself that at least they might have the chance to die together."

Fenn paused, once again gazing at the ocean, while Neita waited impatiently for him to go on. As if sensing her tenseness, Zier pressed against her legs and she absently stroked the dog's head.

"Time seemed to stand still for the woman," Fenn continued, "as she edged fearfully between the trees, not knowing where or when the beast might attack, but knowing it *would*. Only the memory of their love kept her from fleeing back to the village. Finally she came to a small glade, a tiny clearing ringed by the giants of the forest, the ancient trees where the Lieshui dwelt. Moonlight turned the glade as silver as the sword she carried, making her realize she'd been led by the forest spirits to the glade.

"On trembling legs, she stumbled into the clearing and there, too frightened to pray, she waited for the beast that had once been the man she was to marry. As she listened to the murmur of the night wind in the treetops—or was it the Lieshui whispering among themselves?—her resolve almost failed her."

Fenn turned to Neita again, his green eyes staring into hers. "Then, as suddenly as a lightning bolt strikes, the beast appeared before her, a huge, dark menace of claws and fangs. Instead of attacking, he waited, as though longing for the quick and deadly bite of the silver blade. She raised the sword, but despite the horror she faced, she couldn't bring herself to slice down with the blade. He may have been changed into a beast, but part of him was still the man she loved. As the trees rustled all around them, she flung the sword aside and opened her arms to accept the death she knew awaited her.

"When she felt the painful wrenching begin within her, she understood that the Lieshui were granting her mercy in their own strange fashion. Within moments, not one but two beasts, a male and a female, stood side by side in the center of the glade."

Fenn took a deep breath when he finished. "Uncle Theo told the story to us one time and never again," he said, "but I never forgot it and neither did the twins. How could we when he ended the tale with this zinger? 'It is said in Russia that the offspring of those two cursed by the Lieshui was the beginning of the Volan line.'"

Neita, stunned by the power of the story, remained silent, even though Fenn's intent gaze probed for her reaction. A fairy tale, he'd called it. Like all fairy tales, truth lay buried deep within it.

"Theo can't actually believe the tale literally," she said finally. "I'm sure he didn't mean for the three of you to, either."

"Who knows what Theo believes or what he intended?" Fenn asked. "My uncle's always been an enigma."

"What do *you* believe the story means?" she asked.

He looked away from her. At the same time, Zier stopped leaning against Neita's legs and wandered a few steps away to sniff at a dead branch. Had the dog been trying to protect her? Neita wondered. Against Fenn? If so, what made Zier decide her protection was no longer needed?

"Shall we go on?" Fenn asked instead of answering Neita's question about the Russian tale. "What I want to show you isn't too far from here." He didn't wait for her nod before starting off.

She trailed him, preoccupied with the notion there'd been something in Fenn's recounting of his uncle's story that she should have homed in on. What was it? She couldn't bring it to mind.

"Here we are," Fenn announced after a time, stopping near the edge and gesturing with a flourish to the rock face that dropped steeply to the ocean below. Neita halted and stared down. The cliff, while not as precipitous at this spot, was still too sheer for her comfort. At its bottom, she could see a small, rock-strewn beach.

"If you look closely you can see the notches cut into the rock to provide access to the beach," he said.

Examining the cliff face, Neita shook her head. "I see them, but couldn't you have cut bigger steps as long as you were at it?"

"We didn't cut the notches, we found them." As he spoke, he eased over the edge, facing her, his feet searching for and finding what she thought were completely inadequate holds.

"Want to go down?" he asked.

"No! And I hope you won't."

"You're not as intrepid as I thought."

"I'm not rash, either. Why should I risk my neck to climb down to that beach? To prove I'm not afraid to? No, thanks. I freely admit the very thought of making the attempt scares the hell out of me."

He grinned up at her, his toes still tucked into the notches, his elbows resting nonchalantly on the cliff top. "*Ni visovivatsa* means 'Don't lean out.'"

"Very appropriate—you picked a good name. Now that you've proved your point, and made me confess I'm a coward besides, please come up onto the cliff top again before my nerves get the better of me. Doesn't it bother you in any way to hang over the edge like that?"

"If you mean because I fell off another cliff in the mountains, no, that doesn't influence my feeling here. Maybe because I have no memory of the fall. But for your sake, I'll quit hanging over the edge." He lifted himself to the top and scrambled to his feet to stand next to her.

"Did the three of you climb down there often to swim when you were kids?" she asked.

"I may have exaggerated a bit. A couple of times is all. It actually is a hairy descent and when you get to the bottom, the current's too treacherous for swimming. Then you have to climb up again because there's no other choice. As I recall we dared one another into doing it the first time. Lycia was always goading Weslin and me into taking risks by taking them first herself. We couldn't let a girl surpass us."

Again Neita felt the sense of loss she'd experienced before when Fenn spoke of growing up with his cousins. As an only child she'd had no one in her household to play with, vie with, fight with and feel close to.

"I miss those days," he said wistfully. "Since we became adults things aren't the same. Weslin and Lycia aren't the same. And I suppose I'm not, either. Uncle Theo's the only one who remains a constant—I don't suppose I'll ever completely understand him."

Because it had been troubling her, she asked, "Do you really think he was responsible for the Reynolds's trip to Disneyland?"

"Isn't it obvious that he wanted Robbie safely away during the full moon?" Fenn glanced up to the sun shining in an all but cloudless sky. "Tonight," he added, as though she needed to be reminded. "You ought be in Disneyland with them."

All the sunshine in the world couldn't brighten the darkness in her mind when she envisioned the beast howling under the moon as it watched and waited. Not for her, she assured herself. Nothing could or would lure her from the safety of Halfmoon House once night fell.

"I'm not a risk-taker like Lycia," she said tartly.

Fenn raised his eyebrows. "I seem to remember otherwise."

"That's different. You were my patient—I was responsible for you, and so it was my job to go looking for you."

"I'm no longer your patient—keep that in mind." He turned away from her to stare at the ocean. She followed his gaze.

Though the sun glimmered on the blue water near shore, the horizon was obscured by a grayness, the ever-waiting fog bank that almost always hovered off the northern coast. But fog was not her enemy; she had nothing to fear from the fog. Nor from Fenn.

But she feared *for* him. Enough to be bold. "I think we ought to sleep in the same bed tonight so you can't sleepwalk without rousing me," she told him.

He shook his head.

"Are you rejecting the idea or me?" she persisted.

"I don't intend to sleep tonight. And you're far safer with Zier than you'd ever be with me."

She was determined to drag each and every one of his fears, as well as hers, into the open. "Why? Because you believe you're suddenly going to change shape from human to beast?"

He put an arm over her shoulders and drew her away from the cliff, toward the pines that had been twisted into grotesque shapes from braving the sea wind. There they sat side by side on the carpet of brown needles, Zier lying at Neita's feet.

"The beast who comes to call me when the moon is full knows what I am," he said. "I've been certain of that from the first time I heard it howl." He frowned. "Oddly enough, last night I had a sudden conviction that this has happened to me before. By before I mean previous to my accident, before I came to convalesce at Uncle Theo's."

"Are you saying you regained a lost memory?"

He shrugged. "I think so, but, damn it, the amnesia persists, so how can I be sure? Still, I have the feeling the beast came to me somewhere and sometime before the accident."

"In the mountains," she said slowly, "if the same beast drove you over the edge of that cliff, that would mean it's been stalking you."

"I've come to the same conclusion. And, if it's a shapeshifter, maybe I didn't make that trip to the mountains alone."

Neita stared at him. "But what—I mean, who—?" She broke off, uneasy with what she was thinking. How could she believe in humans who changed into beasts? On the other hand, if she refused to believe, she and Fenn might be in even greater danger.

Leaning toward him, she whispered, "I wish—" Again she paused. What was it she wished for?

He smiled one-sidedly. "You wish you'd never met me, right?"

"Wrong!" Meeting him had given her memories to treasure for the rest of her life. She wished for the impossible—that she could be whole again with a Fenn no longer haunted by a menace, both from without and, due to his ancestry, also from within.

He brushed her lips with his forefinger. "Don't try to follow me tonight," he said.

Alarm tensed her. "You can't mean to leave the house after dark!" she cried.

"I don't intend to, but we both know that doesn't mean I won't."

Evidently alerted by Neita's raised voice, Zier's head came up and she glanced from her to Fenn and back.

"There must be a way to lock yourself in so you can't get out, no matter what," Neita said.

"Like the vault? It has occurred to me. I even went to take a look at the vault the other morning when you were still sleeping, but I found the steel door in the basement locked, just as it always used to be. Barnes says there are two keys—Uncle Theo's and a spare that Theo asked him to keep hidden. He said he'd have to check with my uncle before giving me the spare key. So far Barnes hasn't reported back to me.''

"Maybe Theo keeps valuables in the vault."

Fenn shook his head. "He has a bank safety deposit box plus a wall safe in his bedroom suite. Why would he use the vault?"

She had no answer.

He smiled. "Have I ruined your vision of the vault as holding hidden treasure? To tell the truth, I was rather disappointed myself the one and only time I saw the inside of the place. As I told you, it's a small cement room with a drain in the center of the floor and a steel door. No windows, no running water, no electricity. And it's completely underground.

Neita frowned. "But from what your uncle told me, I got the impression that, before his accident, the vault was his private place."

"I know he used to go there sometimes, but I never knew why."

"Maybe he needed the darkness and silence to meditate," Neita said, recalling that both she and Theo had used meditation before she'd called on her healing power to help him.

Fenn shrugged. "Only Theo knows."

Zier had watched them discuss the vault. Now, as if concluding the discussion was over and it was time to go, she got to her feet. Fenn rose and extended a hand to Neita.

"Back to the house?" she asked as he pulled her up.

"I'd rather continue our walk."

"As your uncle mentioned, I can use the exercise," she said.

Fenn turned away from the sea cliffs, following a trail that led across a grassy meadow, through a stand of young evergreens and then down a gradual slope that brought them to cultivated land, presently lying fallow.

"This is part of the Reynolds's farm," he said. "Their house is beyond that rise."

She watched Zier sniff a clod of dirt and then a fence post. Suddenly the dog froze, staring intently at a thickly entwined clump of blackberry vines. What did Zier see? Neita was about to put her hand on Fenn's arm to get his attention when a rabbit burst from the tangle of vines and dashed frantically, in zigzag hops, away from them.

Zier took off after the rabbit but stopped before going far, turning and trotting back to them.

"Smart dog," Neita said. "She's realized that her chances of catching that rabbit were zilch, so why waste the effort?"

"I think she remembered her primary job is to protect you," Fenn said.

As my primary job is to look after you, Neita told herself silently. Even if you *have* resigned as my patient.

In an effort to banish her growing apprehension, she tried to initiate an ordinary conversation. "Do you realize you've never told me what it is you do?" she said. "I know Weslin and Lycia are lawyers, but I haven't the slightest idea what your profession might be."

"I'm a geologist," he said. "I seem to have a talent for homing in on the secrets hidden beneath the earth's surface. Too bad I can't do the same with my own hidden secrets.''

So much for changing the subject, she told herself with a sigh.

When they left the farm, they hiked up the private road toward Halfmoon House, and soon she had little breath left for any talk.

''I swear this is steeper than it used to be,'' Fenn said.

''Let's give me and that newly mended leg of yours a short rest,'' she suggested.

He glanced at his watch and shook his head. ''We're about to miss lunch as it is. I want to get back.''

Fenn didn't speak again before they reached the house. Neita, winded by the climb, also said nothing. Theo was just rolling off the elevator, so lunch hadn't yet been served.

Again, Lycia didn't appear at the table. Neita expected Theo to comment, but he didn't. Maybe because he'd visited Lycia earlier and realized she wasn't up to eating yet. No one had much to say—not even Weslin, who was usually talkative.

Theo looked much the same as he had when she saw him at breakfast, though he was having more difficulty than usual handling his fork with his gloved hands. She'd held his hands without the gloves, but couldn't bring back exactly how they'd felt in hers because the healing had taken all her attention. *Leathery* was what occurred to her.

After they finished and left the table, Fenn took her aside and said, ''Shall we both take a nap?'' His hand lingered on her shoulder. ''Separately, that is, or sleeping isn't what will happen.''

A nap? Neita eyed him suspiciously. Did he really need the rest or was he planning a ruse to elude her watchfulness?

"As I told you when we were at the sea cliffs, I don't plan to sleep tonight," he continued. "So it's now or never."

Shall I trust him? she asked herself. Zier would be with her. Between the two of them they ought to be more than a match for whatever scheme he might have in mind. "I'll leave the connecting door open," she warned.

"Why not?"

Once upstairs, they separated. Neita waited a few minutes, then glanced through the open door and saw Fenn sprawled on his bed with his eyes closed. So far, so good. She had no intention of lying down. Instead, she seated herself in the rocker with Zier at her feet. When repeated trips to the door kept showing an apparently sleeping Fenn, she allowed herself to relax.

Neita rocked quietly as she thought over all that had been said and all that had happened since she'd come to Halfmoon House. She had, she felt, all the pieces, and if she could understand how they fit together, she'd know what to do.

First of all, Theo had recruited her because he sensed her healing power. He also believed she had powers she wasn't using. If he was right, what could those powers be? She cast her mind into the past, to the days when her grandmother was alive, and tried to recall every word Grandma Metsula had ever said to her.

"Your mother was against the name, but I prevailed," her grandmother had told her. "You were born on a night when fog shrouded the land, born on a night when Terhen Neiti drifted across the sky. Your name is proof you're her spirit daughter. Don't take advantage, but if you're in true need, call on the Fog Maiden and she will come."

As Terhen Neiti had done once before to warn her? And perhaps another time to save her. Would she have plunged from the window with Patrick and be dead now if she hadn't begged the Fog Maiden for help?

As she pondered this, Zier's head came up, her muzzle pointed toward the connecting door. Neita was poised to rise when she heard Lycia's voice, pitched a bit too low for her to make out the words. She decided not to look in on them. What went on between Fenn and his cousin was none of her business.

Though she longed to hear what was being said, she forced herself to wait, trying not to count every minute that passed.

Eventually she was rewarded for her reluctant courtesy when Fenn poked his head around the doorframe and saw her sitting demurely—and out of earshot—in the rocker.

"I'll be with Lycia for a while," he said. "See you later."

Since she could hardly ask him where he was going with his cousin, she merely nodded. "I'm glad Lycia's feeling better," she said.

Making no reply, he disappeared from her view. She paused long enough so that she didn't appear to be following him before venturing downstairs with Zier, and was in time to see, through the entry window,

Fenn's sports car zip along the drive with Lycia sitting beside him in the passenger seat.

For no reason she could bring to mind, apprehension trickled icily down Neita's spine. Because Lycia was with Fenn? She shook her head. Lycia was no threat to Fenn, so why be upset?

But she couldn't shrug off her sense of something awry. She was plagued by the feeling she'd overlooked an important detail about Lycia. An image of Tiger formed in her mind and she frowned. What did the cat have to do with Lycia? Was it somehow connected with Robbie?

The boy had kept insisting there was a "'nother lady" on the night he'd vanished from his home. Marianne had believed Robbie must be remembering Lycia's visit earlier on that same evening—but what if Marianne was wrong?

Goose bumps raised on Neita's arms. As if in response to her uneasiness, Zier growled.

CHAPTER FIFTEEN

"Fenn's taking my sister into town." Weslin's voice made Neita jump. Engrossed in trying to recall all that had happened during the night Robbie was missing, she hadn't heard anyone come up behind her in the entry.

When she turned, she noticed Zier was between her and Weslin and she belatedly realized the dog's growl had been a warning. Did Zier feel she needed to be guarded from all the Volans?

"I've got an absolutely blinding headache," Weslin went on, "or I'd have driven Lycia in myself. She needed a few necessities, but she wasn't sure she was well enough to take the car herself. You don't happen to have a miracle headache drug in your nursing supplies, do you?"

"Sorry, just the old standbys," she said. "Have you tried an ice bag?"

"Good idea. I'll see Emily."

As Neita watched him go off toward the kitchen, she berated herself for getting worked up over nothing more than Fenn driving Lycia into town on an errand in broad daylight. She'd certainly overreacted. Just as Zier seemed to be doing. Maybe she was transferring her jumpiness to the dog. Perhaps taking Zier for a brisk walk around the grounds would help them both to calm down.

After returning to the house and finding no one downstairs, Neita went to her room. She was startled to see a small, old leatherbound book lying on her bed, a book that hadn't been there earlier. She picked it up and her eyebrows raised as she glanced at the title: *The Were-wolf*. She'd never heard of the author, Clemence Houseman.

When she opened the slim volume she saw the book had been published in 1896 and that it wasn't a collection of so-called facts about werewolves, as she'd expected, but a story. She was certain the book must have come from Theo's shelves in the tower and that he'd been the one who put it on her bed. Apparently he had a reason for wanting her to read this particular tale.

Settling into the rocker, she began, handling the book's fragile pages with care. After the first paragraph, she became engrossed in the story of a Norse family in a long-ago winter, smiling at the antics of little Rol, the youngest of the household, as he teased old Tyr, the wolfhound.

The mood of the tale altered in a subtle, sinister recounting of a mysterious stranger, a woman who appeared on the family's doorstep, asking shelter from the chill winter night. White Fell, as she called herself, was clad in white furs and she was so fair she won little Rol's heart.

Neita frowned as she read how White Fell sat the child on her knee and kissed him. White Fell vanished from her room that night, and later little Rol disappeared, never to be seen again. Neita stopped reading abruptly.

Sitting with the book in her hands, Neita stared unseeing at its pages, remembering Fenn's account of his aunt Hensa and little Donny. Is that why Theo had put the book in her room? Or did he have an additional reason? She thought of Lycia's visit to the Reynolds farm and how Robbie had reportedly been enthralled with her. The parallel was too obvious to miss.

While she could accept that Lycia might have lured Robbie from the house that night for some unknown reason—she'd been groping toward that conclusion on her own—she wasn't ready to cast Lycia in the role of White Fell. But if Lycia had lured Robbie outside, what had been her motive? Was she planning to bring Robbie to the grounds of Halfmoon House to implicate Fenn? Or had Lycia led the sleepwalking Fenn to the pine grove where Robbie, lost and frightened, waited? If so, what had she expected Fenn to do?

Neita shook her head. Though she sensed she was on the right track, nothing quite made sense. She resumed reading and, once caught up in the heartwrenching story, kept on to the finish. When she closed the book and glanced at the clock, she was amazed to see it was after five. She sprang to her feet, annoyed at herself for not watching the time. Hearing a car outside, she hurried downstairs, hoping it was Fenn returning.

There wasn't a soul to be found on the first floor except Emily, busy in the kitchen.

"The car?" Emily repeated when Neita asked. "That was Barnes taking Mr. Theo to pick up a special order of some kind. I'm fixing a cold supper 'cause Mr. Theo wasn't sure when they'd be back and my friend's picking me up at six this evening to take me to spend the weekend with her in Ferndale. I don't get away real often, so I'm looking forward to it."

"I thought maybe Fenn and Lycia had returned," Neita said.

"I don't think so. At least, I didn't hear the car and I haven't seen them. Mr. Weslin's gone, too. He went for a walk about an hour ago. Didn't tell me where to, or whether he meant to come back for supper."

Zier whined, scratching at the back door to be let out. Neita snapped on the leash and opened the door.

"I sure hope somebody gets back before I leave," Emily said, "'cause I don't like to think of you all alone here. You've got the dog, though—that's some comfort."

Zier might be a comfort, Neita thought as the dog pulled her along, but that didn't help her uneasiness over Fenn. If all Lycia meant to do was pick up a few necessities in town, what was taking them so long? The October days were getting shorter; soon it would be dark. The moon rose early these nights, and tonight the moon would be full....

As they rounded a corner of the house, she saw Weslin striding toward her. At the same time, Zier stopped straining ahead and dropped back to press close to Neita's side.

"Was that Uncle Theo I saw in the car with Barnes?" Weslin asked when he came up to her.

She nodded. "Theo's gone and Fenn and Lycia aren't back yet."

"Are you and I to have dinner tête-à-tête?"

"Emily says it's a cold supper so we may as well wait for the others."

"I'd prefer eating *á deux*," he said, smiling, his amber eyes aglow.

"*Trois*, actually, since Zier insists on staying close to me," she reminded him.

He sighed. "Nothing is ever quite perfect. Don't you find that to be true?"

"I don't expect perfection." She switched the subject to what was on her mind. "What do you think can be taking Fenn so long?"

"I haven't a clue. With Lycia not her usual healthy self, I thought they'd be home long ago. Maybe she decided to see a doctor. You, of all people, should know how much time that can take. Or it's possible they might have had trouble with the car."

"I'm worried," she admitted.

"Tell you what. If they're not home by dark, I'll run into town in my car and try to find them while you and Zier hold down the fort here. Meanwhile, let's grab a bite to eat. Quite frankly, I'm starved."

With no reason to refuse, Neita had little choice but to agree, even though she didn't feel a bit hungry. When they entered the house through the back door, Emily, overnight case in hand, was on her way to the front door.

"I'll just wait on the steps for my friend," she said. "I've got everything ready for supper—you two help yourselves."

The food was set out buffet-style in the dining room, so Neita was able to put a minimum amount on her plate. She noted with some surprise that Weslin, for all his complaint of starving, didn't take much more than she did. She was about to sit down when she heard a car and her heart lifted. Fenn!

Weslin glanced from the window. "Emily's friend," he announced.

Neita concealed her sigh, sat down and began to pick at her food.

"You're neglecting woman's best friend," Weslin chided, gesturing at the dog. "She may never have learned how to sit up and beg, but her eyes certainly know how to plead for a handout."

"Barnes said she wasn't to eat anything except dog food," Neita said defensively.

"The man's heartless. And so are you if you can resist those soulful eyes." He peered at his plate and shook his head. "I agree cold cuts might disagree with Zier, but Emily must have some raw meat in the refrigerator." Rising, he left the room.

While he was gone, Neita gave up all pretense of eating, watching the light coming through the windows fade little by little while her apprehension grew stronger and stronger.

Weslin returned with several chunks of raw beef. Zier needed no persuasion to gulp down every last morsel and look around for more, but Neita was too upset to pay much attention.

"Weslin," she said, "I really think something must have happened to Fenn and Lycia. And it *is* getting dark."

"I'm a bit worried myself," he told her. "As you said, the food can wait. I'll go immediately. Make sure the doors are locked, okay?"

She heaved a sigh of relief that he was finally moved to take action. Whether he could find them or not was something else again—but at least he'd be trying.

Weslin hadn't been gone from the house five minutes before she heard a car in the drive. Was he returning for some reason? She dashed to the entry in
time to see Theo's silver car pass by. Disappointed that
it wasn't Fenn, but glad she wouldn't be alone, she
hurried to the kitchen, knowing Theo would use the
back door because there were no steps to hinder his
wheelchair.

"Weslin's gone after Fenn and Lycia," she told
Theo, walking alongside his wheelchair as he rolled
toward the entry. Barnes trailed behind, carrying a
long package.

Theo nodded, his face grim. "I saw his car and had
Barnes flag him down."

"Do you think—"

"I haven't time to talk, Neita." He rolled past her
and into the elevator, Barnes following him. As the
doors closed, Theo called, "Stay inside!"

He left Neita feeling more alone than ever. Even the
dog seemed to have deserted her. Where had Zier gotten to? Before she started to look for the Doberman,
she heard a car pull up in the front of the house, ran
to the entry window and saw Weslin slide from the
driver's side and hurry around to the other side. When
she realized he was helping someone from the car, she
flung open the front door. As she watched Weslin, she
became aware that the moon was rising above the
trees.

"I found Lycia," he said as he half carried his sister up the steps and into the entry. Lycia, wrapped
from head to foot in something dark, stumbled into

the small bathroom off the entry and closed herself inside.

"What's wrong—" Neita began.

"She'll be all right," Weslin said. "It's Fenn we have to rescue."

Neita bit her lip. "Do you know where he is?"

"I'm afraid I do." Weslin spoke as though each word was being forced from his throat. "Lycia told me he's locked himself in the vault."

She stared at Weslin, unable to take in what he was saying. "But how did he get to the vault? Where's his car?"

"Lycia says they ran out of gas on the way home. He managed to pull off the road into the Reynolds's farm, where he abandoned both her and the car. He said he couldn't wait, that he had to shut himself away from everyone, and the vault was the only safe place. I don't know how to say this, but—" Weslin hesitated, his face grim "—Fenn wasn't exactly himself by then. Poor Lycia was scared out of her wits. After Fenn loped off, she left the car and tackled the hill on foot. Weak as she is, it took her forever to get even halfway up. That's where I found her."

Fear for Fenn roiled inside Neita, but one thing still wasn't clear to her. "But—but how is it you were able to find your sister?"

"Lycia's my twin. There's a special sixth sense between us."

Identical twins could have a flow of mental telepathy between them, Neita knew. Quite possibly some fraternal twins might, as well.

"There's no time to waste," Weslin said urgently. "We must get to the vault. Fenn's so disturbed I'm afraid he'll go mad if he stays in that damnable place. Imagine being locked in a prison cell in the dark." Weslin shuddered.

Neita clenched her fists as she visualized Fenn shut away underground. He'd told her about asking Barnes for the key, but she hadn't really believed Fenn would choose the vault as the answer to his fears.

"I wouldn't ask you to come along," Weslin said, "but Fenn might not listen to me. Lycia said he'd do anything for you and I know she's right. Please help me."

"Yes," she said. "Yes, I will. Let's hurry!"

The steps leading to the basement were off the kitchen. Recalling that Barnes kept a battery lantern hanging on a hook beside the dog's leash, she paused long enough to grab it before following Weslin. As she descended the steep stairs, she realized how easy it would be to make a false step and could understand why Theo had fallen here.

A bare light bulb dangling from a cord in the middle of the room provided scant illumination. Jars of fruit preserves sat on storage shelves at the foot of the stairs. Otherwise there was little to be seen except a hot-water heater and a furnace.

Weslin crossed the basement, inserted a key in a steel door and opened it. He flicked a switch inside the door, but no lights went on.

"The bulbs must be burned-out," he said, switching on his flashlight.

She turned on her lantern and, by its light, saw a cement corridor stretching into darkness. A dank, faintly unpleasant odor drifted into the basement through the open door. She wrinkled her nose, frowning because the smell seemed vaguely familiar, but she couldn't identify what it was.

As she followed Weslin into what she remembered Fenn had called a tunnel, it belatedly occurred to her to wonder about the key Weslin had used. She recalled that Fenn had said the same key opened both steel doors, but where had Weslin's key come from?

"I thought there were only two keys to these doors," she said.

"That's right. I have the spare key."

"Then Fenn must have Theo's key. I'm surprised Theo would give his key to Fenn."

"Fenn might simply have taken it."

She thought for a moment. "Since you do have a key, you can unlock the vault door as well as this one. So why do you think we'll have a problem getting Fenn out?"

"What if he refuses? I fully expect him to—that's why you're with me. To persuade him."

Neita had to agree Weslin was right. Fenn might be hard to convince. She lifted the lantern to see if there were spiderwebs hanging from the low ceiling of the cement tunnel. She saw none. Maybe because even insects shunned the place. She didn't blame them.

Though she wasn't exactly frightened, she didn't like the closed-in feeling of the tunnel, and she wished Zier was beside her. Where *was* the dog?

The sweetish smell grew stronger and the air colder. "How long is this tunnel?" she asked Weslin.

"Twenty feet or so. The dark makes it seem longer. Here's the end now." The beam of his flashlight gleamed dully on the second steel door.

Her heart thudded as he inserted the key and turned it. He grasped the latch and the door swung inward silently, liberating a noisome stench, so foul that she gagged.

"Oh my God!" Weslin cried.

Holding her breath against the smell, Neita eased next to him. What she saw in the glare of his flashlight shocked her so profoundly that the lantern fell from her nerveless hand. A decomposing body lay a few feet inside the vault, a man many weeks dead.

"It's—it's Jethro." Weslin's words were muffled by the hand he'd clapped over his mouth. "My God, Fenn, what have you done?"

Neita stared helplessly at the dead man, unable to move or speak.

At that moment, a long ululating howl echoed along the corridor.

The beast! Terror raised the hair on her nape.

"The only safe place is inside the vault." Weslin shoved her forward as he spoke, his voice gruff—no doubt with fright.

Unable to catch herself, she stumbled over the dropped lantern and through the open door. Before she had a chance to do or say anything, the door clanged shut and, in complete darkness she heard the key turn. Weslin had locked them inside the vault with Jethro's body.

"Turn on the flashlight," she begged him, shuddering.

There was no answer.

"Weslin?" she said. "Weslin!"

Long minutes later, she realized the truth. Weslin had locked the vault door—but from the outside. She was alone, trapped in the vault with the dead.

CHAPTER SIXTEEN

Caught in the merciless claws of unreasoning terror, Neita banged on the steel door with her fists, screaming and crying, begging incoherently for help. At last, temporarily spent, she fell to her knees, her forehead resting against the cold metal of the door.

Slowly, bit by bit, her mind began to function again. Soundproof room. Shouting's useless. Steel door. Can't break through. Jethro's dead. He can't hurt you. No light. No harm in darkness.

When the next wave of panic began to crest—have to get out, havetogetout, getoutgetout—she curled herself into a ball and fought against being swept into mindlessness again. Finally she was able to sit up and hug herself, shivering from the chill of the room as well as her residual fear. The smell was no longer quite so overpowering, probably because she'd adapted to the stench, but she wasn't able to forget how close she was to Jethro's body.

While he wasn't the first dead person she'd ever seen, death in the clean confines of a hospital wasn't the same as sharing this horrible dark cell with a decomposing body.

Aware she must remain rational, she banished the thought of Jethro and closed her eyes, choosing her own darkness to that inside the vault. Meditation offered her the only escape possible, but never had she found it more difficult to blank her mind.

When at last the healing light poured into her, Neita relaxed, unaware, for the moment, of her surroundings. Without conscious thought, she used her renewed energy to send a silent appeal for help.

Vaguely aware someone was calling him, Fenn struggled up from profound inner darkness to the moonlit darkness of reality. For a time he didn't understand the difference. Gradually his mind began to function and he realized he was lying on his back somewhere outside. At night. Under the full moon. Where was he? What had happened?

When he sat up, the world whirled dizzily around him and he was attacked by acute nausea. Twisting to one side, he vomited onto the grass. When the retching ended, his dizziness eased and he pushed himself to his feet. He stood unsteadily, head pounding, and tried to recall what had brought him to wherever he was.

After his balance felt secure, he looked around, half expecting to see the firs and pines of the mountains. Instead, the unmistakable outline of a barn loomed before him. The Reynolds barn, he realized after a moment's concentration. He was at their farm—but how had he gotten here?

His thoughts were inexplicably fuzzy, but he did remember being in a car. With someone. Neita? As her name sprang into his mind, an image of her face appeared, seeming to hang in the air in front of him, her eyes imploring, her lips parted in a silent appeal. An instant later the image was gone, but her soundless cry for help lingered.

Neita was in danger. She needed him. Where was she? He didn't know, but Halfmoon House was the most likely place. He had to find her, had to help her.

A car would be the fastest, and he knew he'd been in his car. But where was it? He started to turn away from the barn when a glimmer of moonlight on metal caught his eye, so he stumbled toward the barn rather than toward the road.

He found his car at the far side of the barn in deep shadow, except for where the moon's rays touched one end of the rear bumper. But the keys weren't in the ignition, and when he searched his pockets, the keys weren't there, either.

Lycia. She'd been the one in the car with him. He'd driven her into Eureka and she'd dallied in one store or another until he'd lost all patience and insisted they had to get back. Then on the way home she'd inveigled him into stopping for coffee at a doughnut shop. She'd gone in and brought out two containers. His coffee had been so bitter he'd left half.

Then what? Something about a cat. Yes, that was it. He hadn't seen one, but as they neared the Reynolds farm, she claimed to have spotted Tiger in the drive.

"They've gone away and left the poor cat," Lycia had said. "We can't let him go hungry. Do turn in." She'd grabbed the wheel and turned the car herself.

He'd been a bit groggy by then. Taken by surprise, he hadn't been able to wrest control of the car from her, and they'd swerved into the Reynolds's drive. And then—? Fenn shook his head, recalling no more until he woke up on the ground with the moon shining down on him.

What the hell was Lycia up to, abandoning him here and taking the car keys? And why had he passed out? All he'd had since lunch was the coffee.

Coffee that Lycia had given him. Reluctant as he was to believe she'd put something into the coffee, he was forced to admit she must have. Because he'd been drugged. Nothing else could explain what had happened to him—the blackout, the dizziness, the vomiting. And the headache. She'd drugged him and deliberately stranded him here.

Why?

What was going on at Halfmoon House? He spun around and broke into a shambling run, cursing his sluggish reflexes. Neita had called on the bond between them and summoned him, he was certain. He must go to her!

On foot, the path up through the pine grove to the sea cliffs would be quicker than taking the road. Damn it, what devilish scheme did Lycia have in mind? If she dared to harm Neita . . .

A howl, high-pitched and quavering, raised his hackles and set his teeth on edge. The beast! He remembered the black cape in the church ruins, a cape such as Lycia's mother, his aunt Hensa, had worn, and his steps faltered as shock juddered through him. No, he told himself. Impossible!

But in his heart of hearts he knew—and feared—the truth.

* * *

In the vault, Neita stood leaning dispiritedly against the steel door. For a brief second she'd had a sensation of contact with Fenn, but the moment had passed so quickly she feared she'd imagined it.

Though her ear was pressed against the metal, she could hear nothing from the other side. The door shut away sounds from her, as well as keeping her cries for help from being heard. Even if her loudest shout could penetrate the door, only someone who was already in the tunnel would hear her, and she was all but certain the tunnel was deserted.

Now that she could think again, she realized Weslin had deliberately lured her to the vault so he could lock her inside. But why hadn't Zier followed them? Neita clenched her fists as she realized Weslin must have done something to prevent Zier from trailing after her. She thought of the chunks of raw meat he'd fed Zier and grimaced. He must have concealed something in the meat to eliminate the dog. Zier would have been an obstacle to his plans. Whatever they might be.

For a few moments Neita forgot her own desperate plight in her worry over Zier. Whatever Weslin had given the dog must have been quick-acting because she realized now that Zier had never left the dining room. She fervently hoped Zier was still alive, hoped that Weslin had drugged rather than fatally poisoning the poor dog.

Though she fought against falling into the despair of believing she would never be set free—why had Weslin imprisoned her?—the grim possibility lurked in the depths of her mind. She tried not to think of

Jethro and failed dismally. How long had he been locked in this vault before he died? she wondered. But then, recalling her glimpse of his naked, blood-smeared body, she shook her head. Jethro hadn't died of hunger and thirst.

Had the beast killed him? If so, who'd concealed the body in the vault? The werewolf in human form? The possibility piled fear upon fear.

When at last she heard the faint click of metal against metal and identified the sound as a key being inserted in the lock of the vault door, her heart leapt. Fenn, coming to her rescue! Almost immediately, fear gripped her by the throat. More likely Weslin returning. She held little hope he meant to let her go, but she wanted her freedom so desperately that she'd rather face a new threat than stay locked in the vault.

The key turned and the door swung open. Blinded by the beam of a flashlight, Neita couldn't see who stood in the tunnel. "F-Fenn?" she said falteringly, hoping against hope.

"It's Barnes. Are you all right?"

As she stumbled through the opening, the light swung away from her, focusing on the interior of the vault. Barnes drew in his breath and began to retch. She caught his arm, trying to pull him with her along the tunnel, her only thought to flee from the vault as fast as she could.

The door to the basement had been left open, and a dark shape was framed against the light slanting through—a four-footed shape. Neita halted, the taste of fear metallic on her tongue.

Then she heard a whine, the animal lurched toward her, and she understood what it was she saw. Not the beast. Zier. Dropping to her knees, she threw her arms around the dog.

"For God's sake, let's get out of here," Barnes muttered, urging her to her feet again.

Moments later, Neita, Barnes and Zier stood in the basement, the steel door locked behind them. Barnes, his face ghastly in the feeble light, grabbed Zier's collar, half dragging the dog up the stairs with Neita at his heels.

In the kitchen Theo waited, sitting in a motorized cart rather than his regular wheelchair. "I recognize death's awful smell," he said. "Jethro?"

Barnes nodded, then gagged, clapped his hand over his mouth and rushed from the kitchen. Neita sank down on a kitchen stool, Zier collapsing at her feet.

Theo sighed deeply, a long drawn-out gust of breath. "I fear I've waited too long. But I had to be sure because once I take action, there's no turning back. For any of us."

"How did you know where I was?" she asked.

"We heard the dog crying—there's no other word to describe the sounds she made—and Barnes came down from my bedroom suite to see what was wrong with her. He found Zier staggering across the kitchen toward the basement door. He recognized immediately that she'd been drugged, so he came to tell me.

"When I got here, Zier was pressed against the basement door, whimpering. Since she obviously couldn't navigate the stairs, Barnes carried her down and she dragged herself to the tunnel door. Barnes and

I both knew she had to be following your trail and that you must be in the vault. Barnes used my key to enter—apparently the spare is missing."

"Weslin—" she said, but Theo held up his gloved hand to stop her before she could go on.

"I know the rest," he said wearily, "and there's worse to come. Listen."

She heard the howling then and hugged herself. Zier, groggy as she still was, growled, her hackles raised.

"Not close to the house," Theo said. "Near the sea cliffs, I'd say." He rolled closer and touched her gently on the shoulder. "You've been through one hell. Now I'm asking you to plunge into an even deadlier hell. To save Fenn."

She stared at him, not understanding what he was asking her to do.

"If Fenn resists, he's doomed. If he gives way, he's damned. He has no other choices—unless you can offer him a way to escape. To give him that chance, you must go to the sea cliffs and you must go quickly. Alone. Zier's in no shape to be of help and, even if she were, quite likely she'd be killed."

"And I won't be?" she whispered, shocked by the enormity of what he was asking her to do.

"Not if you can tap your latent power."

She shook her head, aware she had no idea how to use powers she wasn't even sure she possessed.

"If you don't risk yourself," Theo warned, "Fenn will be lost forever."

Intent on her own conflicting emotions, she only vaguely noticed that Theo spoke with effort. She wanted nothing more than to crawl into a safe place and hide, but the despair in Theo's voice held her back.

"You called to Fenn when you were locked in the vault, didn't you?" Theo asked.

Neita blinked in surprise. "Yes."

"He'd have come to you if he possibly could, and you know it. But he's trapped as surely as you were behind that locked door of the vault."

"What about the—the pentagram he saw on my palm?" she faltered. "He said it meant I was his next victim."

Theo's bleak expression lightened a little. "The Russian gypsies say that's a sign two people are meant for one another. That makes Fenn your victim as much as you're his. Go to him, Neita. Help him."

As she pondered Theo's words, a dreadful awareness stabbed into Neita, making her gasp with shock. Somewhere in the moonlit darkness Fenn was in terrible danger and he needed her desperately. The knowledge came from the bond they shared, but was no less real for being intangible.

If she ventured into the night where the beast howled, would she be able to save Fenn? Without him, she'd be but half-alive. Wasn't he worth risking everything for?

She rose from the chair, dimly aware that Zier was struggling to her feet.

"Don't let the dog out," Theo warned her, apparently realizing she'd made up her mind. "And be sure you have your dagger."

Neita touched the pocket of her gray flannel pants where the knife nestled in its sheath. She slipped through the back door, closing it quickly, ignoring Zier's mournful complaint at being left behind.

The sea cliffs, Theo had said. Neita thought of the ruined church and nodded grimly, feeling herself drawn in that direction. The moon laid a silvery path for her feet to follow across the grounds, a beautiful but sinister road that beckoned her toward the evil she sensed in the darkness.

Her hurrying steps faltered when the beast howled again, and she stopped dead when an answering howl rose as the first began to fade away. Two!

Was she already too late? Had Fenn—?

No, she told herself firmly. Don't let your courage fail because of Fenn's mistaken fear that he's a werewolf. You've never sensed any shadow in him—no matter what he believes, he's *not* a shapeshifter.

But that didn't change the terrifying fact that two beasts roamed the night. How could she possibly survive? When she couldn't force herself to go on, in desperation she conjured up one of her grandmother's charms against being afraid:

"Lenna mustilla siivilla," she chanted under her breath.

"Fly on black wings
Away from me, O fear,
Return to Tuonela's dark river.
Leave me, fear,
Fly back to hell's river
On your black and loathsome wings..."

By the time she finished the chant, she found herself no longer paralyzed by fright and able to hurry on past the gazebo toward the sea cliffs. While still afraid, her fear had become an unwelcome companion rather than an opponent trying to prevent her from doing what she must do.

The eerie chorus continued, two beasts howling under the moon, chilling the very marrow of her bones. She eased her silver dagger from its sheath and gripped the hilt tightly, slowing as she approached the cliff, dismayed to see the stone ruins dead ahead. For her the ruins embodied the evil she sensed in the night; she thought of them as the lair of the beasts. Or werebeasts. Humans taking the shape of beasts.

Shapeshifters.

Though she couldn't see the beasts, the howling was very near, so close she halted and searched for a vantage point, a spot where she could defend herself without being attacked from behind. Skirting the ruins, she came to the flat-topped rock split by the pine and scrambled up one side until she found solid footing and could put her back to the pine trunk. The height gave her a panoramic view.

The moon rode a cloudless sky, its pale light illuminating ruins and cliff and ocean, as well as the dark and sinister shapes of two massive beasts. Neita was well aware the moonlight revealed her, too, but neither beast noticed, intent as they were on the man they stalked.

Fenn!

The beasts were between her and Fenn, and they were driving him slowly toward the edge of the cliff. How was she to help him? It seemed impossible....

Fenn, trying to hold his ground against the howling beasts, did his best to block the insistent whispering in his mind. The coaxing murmur came from the smaller of the two beasts, and it sickened him to know who she was.

"Come and be one of us," she urged. "We'll show you the way. Come and be free, run with us under the moon, feel the hot thrill of blood lust. Death lies on the rocks below, but we offer you life as it should be lived. Change, Fenris, change. Shifting's in your blood, let yourself feel the urge, let go and be one with us, be more than human...."

The worst of it was, he could *feel* the urge. Something deep within him responded to her coaxing even while he fought against it. The two of them were deliberately driving him to the edge of the cliff, making him choose between death and...obscene horror. He didn't want to die but he didn't want to be like them— not more than human, but less. Yet the urge grew stronger, grew harder to resist. It would be so easy to stop struggling, to—

Suddenly he sensed another presence close by. Not a beast. Neita! Why had she risked herself by coming here? If he succumbed to the lure and was able to change, he'd not only damn himself but doom her.

Was there any way to save her? To save himself?

If I could recapture my lost memories, he told himself, I might be able resist this sinister compulsion. I'm sure there's a truth hidden under the dark cloak of my amnesia. But how the hell can I make myself remember?

Watching Fenn take yet another backward step, another step closer to the cliff edge, Neita caught her breath. She glanced at the silver dagger in her hand and shook her head. She could never fend off two beasts. Yet she had to act or Fenn would die.

Staring out over the ocean at the ever-present offshore fog bank, she noticed with a thrill of hope that it was nearer shore than usual. Reaching into her innermost self, she sent a silent call.

Terhen Neiti, hear your namesake, hear me and help your human daughter. Come to me in your gray cloak of mist, cover me with your soft gray blanket, hide me from my enemies, from those who would destroy me. Let your gray tentacles coil about them to hinder and confuse them. Be my guide and friend, Fog Maiden.

The fog rolled rapidly in to shore, silent and thick, caressing her with soft gray fingers, wrapping her in a damp embrace. She breathed her thanks to Terhen Neiti as she slid from the split rock, concealed by the heavy gray mist. Though unable to see where she was going, Neita didn't need to. The bond connecting her to Fenn, a radiance she sensed rather than saw, drew her to his side.

Fenn was scarcely aware the moon had vanished before gray mist wrapped so thickly around him that he couldn't see or hear. He struggled against the feeling that the fog was entering his very soul. After a moment, he remembered this was a friend and stopped fighting, welcoming Neita's Fog Maiden, opening himself to her.

Nothing existed except her concealing gray cloak that blanketed even his thoughts. Time had no meaning.

As abruptly as it came, the fog suddenly vanished. Vanishing with it was the gray curtain that had blocked Fenn's memory—the fog of his amnesia was gone.

He found Neita at his side, the two beasts flanking them. But now he remembered everything he'd forgotten. He remembered the camping trip to the mountains with his cousins, remembered how, as the full moon rose over the firs, Lycia had teased and coaxed him into letting her try to hypnotize him.

She'd succeeded, at least in part, because she'd made him believe that sooner or later he must become like the beasts she and Weslin had changed into when the moon climbed the sky. But he hadn't changed that night. He'd fled from the horror of seeing his cousins shape-shift and he'd plunged over the cliff.

He hadn't changed that night, and he knew now he need never change. Would never change.

"They're closing in," Neita warned, bringing him back to their very real danger.

Fenn stared from one to the other of the werebeasts, fixing his gaze on the smaller. She, as always, was the instigator. "Never!" he shouted. "I'll never change!"

When Neita raised her silver dagger, the smaller beast recoiled, and he understood why. Silver was poison and the beast feared it because she'd already been wounded by that knife when she'd attacked Neita. There'd been no party, no alcohol, no hangover. Lycia's recent illness came from being stabbed by a silver dagger.

But she was still a threat, and Weslin even more so. With one small silver dagger their only protection, how could he and Neita hope to survive? Still, he'd do his damnedest to save her. He'd fight to the end.

"I hear a motor," Neita told him.

At that moment both beasts raised their muzzles to the night sky, their hairy bodies silvered by moonlight. They howled in unison, a long, heart-stopping challenge that made Fenn tense for the inevitable onslaught.

"Look!" Neita cried.

The beasts sprang toward them.

Focused on the attack, Fenn scarcely heard the two sharp cracks. He stared in amazement as first the smaller beast, then the larger, dropped in their tracks. Only then did he realize he'd heard shots.

And then he saw Uncle Theo mounted on his motorized cart with a rifle across his knees. Pulling Neita with him, Fenn ran to Theo.

"I made sure," Uncle Theo gasped, one furred hand clutching his chest. "Silver bullets."

"Medicine," Neita cried to Theo. "Where's your medicine?"

He shook his head. "My time's run out. Don't want to live."

Fenn, gazing in shock at his uncle's hairy, taloned hands, whispered, "You're one."

Uncle Theo shook his head. "Used to be. Not since my accident, except for my hands when the moon's full. Had to have the trigger changed so I could fire the rifle. Silver bullets made to order. Gunsmith thought I was crazy."

"When did you realize?" Neita asked.

"Suspected Lycia was a secret shifter for a long time. Think she showed Weslin how to change." He stared at Fenn. "She tried to make you one of them. Couldn't have that. She was sleeping with Jethro—I think she shifted unexpectedly and killed him."

"She tried to kill me," Neita said.

"You stood between her and Fenn. Don't know what she meant to do with Robbie. I sent him away so he'd be safe. Loved the twins. Didn't want to kill them." Tears filled Theo's eyes as he looked at the dead beasts.

Fenn followed his gaze, and blinked. Lycia and Weslin, both naked, lay crumpled on the rocky ground. In death, they'd become human once more.

"We must get you back to the house," Neita told Theo, her voice urgent.

"Wait," Theo insisted. "Fenn, listen. You tell the police I shot the twins in a fit of rage after we found Jethro's body because I knew they'd killed him." He was gasping when he finished.

"You found Jethro?" Fenn asked.

"Neita'll tell you later." He reached a hand to Fenn.

Fenn clasped Theo's malformed hand in his. "You're a Volan but not a shifter," Theo whispered, each word a struggle. "Left letter for you. Read it." He reached his other hand toward Neita, and without hesitation, she grasped it.

Theo brought his hands together, joining Neita's hand with Fenn's. Looking at Neita, he whispered, "Take good care of Fenn—he's the last of the Volans."

EPILOGUE

Alone in her room, Neita laid the last of her belongings into her bag and dropped the lid with a sigh. Fenn had withstood the shock of Theo's death coming so close after that of his cousins remarkably well, but she'd stayed on at Halfmoon House until the investigation and the funerals were over because she felt he needed her by his side.

Now she had no excuse left—it was time for her to go. She was zipping the bag shut when she heard Fenn's shout from downstairs.

"Neita! Where the devil are you?" His voice was laced with urgency.

Stepping into the corridor, she called, "I'm upstairs."

"I need you—hurry! Barnes isn't here and something's wrong with Zier."

Neita ran along the corridor and down the stairs to the entry, where Fenn crouched over Zier. The dog lay sprawled onto the parquet floor near the bottom of the steps as though she'd tried to climb them and collapsed. She was panting, her tongue hanging from her mouth.

Flinging herself onto her knees beside the dog, Neita rested a hand on Zier's head. "What's the matter, girl?" she asked in a soothing tone.

Assured that Zier accepted her touch, Neita ran a hand over the dog's body, checking for possible injuries. She paused when she reached Zier's belly. "I should have guessed," she murmured.

"What is it?" Fenn demanded.

"Zier's in labor."

Fenn's eyebrows rose. "She's *what?*"

"About to give birth. You might ask Emily for an old blanket so Zier will be more comfortable."

Emily brought the blanket herself. "Will wonders never cease," she said, staring down at the dog. "Not a one of us guessed Zier was going to have puppies. Poor old Zorn must have been the father. Just wait till I tell Barnes. He doted on Zorn, never got over the dog being killed in that dreadful way. It'll make a difference, him knowing Zorn died defending his mate *and* his pups." She bustled off.

After coaxing the dog onto the blanket, Neita sat on the floor beside Zier, waiting. Fenn eased down next to her.

"This is a first for me," he said. "I never saw an animal give birth. Theo had neither cats nor dogs when I was growing up."

"Animals tend to have their young with a lot less fuss than humans," Neita told him. "Look, there's the first puppy's head."

While Zier was licking the first pup clean, another arrived. Soon the two pups found nipples and began to nurse. Zier raised her head and glanced at Neita, then Fenn.

"If ever I saw a smug look, that's it," Fenn commented.

"Zier has good reason to be proud. In spite of all she's been through, she's managed to deliver two healthy babies." As Neita spoke she tried to ignore the pang of deprivation she felt.

"I suppose we'll have to fix her a bed in your room," he said, rising. "She isn't content unless you're in sight. She was trying to climb the stairs to get to you when I found her in the entry."

Neita stood because she wanted to be face-to-face with Fenn when she told him. Seeing Zier's anxious look, she shrugged and seated herself on the steps. "You're looming over me," she said to Fenn, putting off what she knew she must say.

He sat beside her, draping an arm over her shoulders.

"No," she protested, sliding away. "Don't." Twisting to face him, she said, "When you called me to come and help Zier, I'd just finished packing. The time's come for me to leave Halfmoon House."

He stared at her as though she was out of her mind. "Leave? Why?"

"You don't really need me here any longer." To her distress, tears pricked her eyes. She blinked them back.

He sprang to his feet, grasped her hands and pulled her up. Gazing into her eyes, he said, "Do you want to go?"

"I—" Her voice broke and the words she tried to say stuck in her throat while her eyes filled with the tears that could no longer be denied.

"I take it the answer is no," he said gruffly.

She bit her lip, fighting to regain her composure. "It's best for both—"

He caught her by the shoulders. "We can't be apart. You know that as well as I do. But I can't blame you for wanting to get away from me now that you've discovered the truth about the Volan heritage. Uncle Theo's letter made it clear we Volans truly carry a curse."

Unable to help herself, needing to touch him, Neita raised her hand to his cheek. "That's not the reason."

"Then, what is? You must know I love you and want to marry you."

His words thrilled through her, melting her heart. "Oh, Fenn," she whispered, laying her head against his chest. "I love you, too."

"There's more," he said. "Not that I'd want to, but the truth is I can't father children, because I had an operation when I was a young teenager. Uncle Theo, fearing what might happen, told the three of us the Volan line carried a rare genetic disorder that would lead to defective children and so we agreed to the surgery. As he said in the letter, he had no choice. I agree."

Tears spilled down Neita's cheeks as she looked up at him. "That doesn't matter. I've been dreading to tell you that I can't ever have a child because of the accident with the glass when Patrick leapt through the window."

He kissed her tenderly, a bonding kiss that held a promise of passion.

"We can adopt children," she murmured against his lips. "Maybe children with disabilities, children who need extra loving care from a mother and father who understand flaws and how to overcome them.''

He raised his head to smile down at her, a loving smile with only a hint of sadness. "Children who'll begin a new line, untainted by the Volan curse.''

His lips met hers again, this time in a deep, torrid kiss that left them both eager for more. As one, they turned and, arms around each other, climbed the stairs.

"I've got this strong feeling that Uncle Theo engineered this from the start,'' Fenn told her as they reached the top. "That he planned all along for us to marry. I have to admit that this time he really had the right idea.''

They entered her room and Fenn was about to close the door when he paused and groaned. "Look," he said.

Neita poked her head through the door. When she saw Zier trotting toward them, carrying one of the puppies in her mouth, she began to laugh.

"There's nothing you can do about it,'' she told Fenn. "This is clearly a classic case of love me, love my dog."

* * * * *

MONTANA MAVERICKS™

Stories that capture living and loving beneath the Big Sky, where legends live on...and the mystery is just beginning.

Watch for the sizzling debut of
MONTANA MAVERICKS in August with

ROGUE STALLION

by Diana Palmer

A powerful tale of simmering desire and mystery!

And don't miss a minute of the loving as the mystery continues with:

THE WIDOW AND THE RODEO MAN
by Jackie Merritt (September)
SLEEPING WITH THE ENEMY
by Myrna Temte (October)
THE ONCE AND FUTURE WIFE
by Laurie Paige (November)
THE RANCHER TAKES A WIFE
by Jackie Merritt (December)
and many more of your favorite authors!

Only from  Silhouette® where passion lives.

MAV1

**Silhouette Books
is proud to present
our best authors, their best books...
and the best in your reading pleasure!**

**Throughout 1994, look for exciting books
by these top names in contemporary
romance:**

DIANA PALMER
Enamored in August

HEATHER GRAHAM POZZESSERE
The Game of Love in August

FERN MICHAELS
Beyond Tomorrow in August

NORA ROBERTS
The Last Honest Woman in September

LINDA LAEL MILLER
Snowflakes on the Sea in September

*When it comes to passion,
we wrote the book.*

BOBQ3

Silhouette®

Fifty red-blooded, white-hot, true-blue hunks
from every State in the Union!

Look for MEN MADE IN AMERICA! Written by some of
our most popular authors, these stories feature fifty of
the strongest, sexiest men, each from a different state in
the union!

Two titles available every other month at your favorite
retail outlet.

In May, look for:

KISS YESTERDAY GOODBYE by Leigh Michaels (Iowa)
A TIME TO KEEP by Curtiss Ann Matlock (Kansas)

In June, look for:

ONE PALE, FAWN GLOVE by Linda Shaw (Kentucky)
BAYOU MIDNIGHT by Emilie Richards (Louisiana)

You won't be able to resist MEN MADE IN AMERICA!

If you missed your state or would like to order any other states that have already been
published, send your name, address, zip or postal code along with a check or money
order (please do not send cash) for $3.59 for July and $3.99 for September for each
book, plus 75¢ postage and handling ($1.00 in Canada), payable to Harlequin Reader
Service, to:

In the U.S.	In Canada
3010 Walden Avenue	P.O. Box 609
P.O. Box 1369	Fort Erie, Ontario
Buffalo, NY 14269-1369	L2A 5X3

Please specify book title(s) with your order.
Canadian residents add applicable federal and provincial taxes.

MEN594R

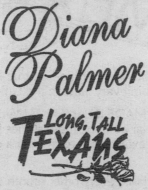

SILHOUETTE®

Desire®

Big Bad WOLFE

WOLFE WATCHING
by Joan Hohl

Undercover cop Eric Wolfe knew *everything* about divorcée Tina Kranas, from her bra size to her bedtime—without ever having spent the night with her! The lady was a suspect, and Eric had to keep a close eye on her. But since his binoculars were getting all steamed up from watching her, Eric knew it was time to start wooing her....

WOLFE WATCHING, Book 2 of Joan Hohl's devilishly sexy Big Bad Wolfe series, is coming your way in July...only from Silhouette Desire.

HE'S AN

AMERICAN HERO

Men of mettle. Men of integrity. Real men who know the real meaning of love. Each month, Intimate Moments salutes these true American Heroes.

For July: THAT SAME OLD FEELING,
by Judith Duncan.
Chase McCall had come home a new man. Yet old lover Devon Manyfeathers soon stirred familiar feelings—and renewed desire.

For August: MICHAEL'S GIFT,
by Marilyn Pappano.
Michael Bennett knew his visions prophesied certain death. Yet he would move the high heavens to change beautiful Valery Navarre's fate.

For September: DEFENDER,
by Kathleen Eagle.
Gideon Defender had reformed his bad-boy ways to become a leader among his people. Yet one habit—loving Raina McKenny—had never died, especially after Gideon learned she'd returned home.

AMERICAN HEROES: Men who give all they've got for their country, their work—the women they love.

Only from

™ Silhouette®

IMHER09